I0562093

THE AGE
of
INNOCENCE

BARBARA MURRELL, ED. D.

Outskirts Press, Inc.
Denver, Colorado

This is a work of fiction. The events and characters described herein are imaginary and are not intended to refer to specific places or living persons. The opinions expressed in this manuscript are solely the opinions of the author and do not represent the opinions or thoughts of the publisher.

The Age of Innocence
All Rights Reserved.
Copyright © 2009 Barbara Murrell, Ed. D.
V6.0 R3.1

Cover Photo © 2009 JupiterImages Corporation. All rights reserved - used with permission.

Author's photographer.: Dannille McGouirk

This book may not be reproduced, transmitted, or stored in whole or in part by any means, including graphic, electronic, or mechanical without the express written consent of the publisher except in the case of brief quotations embodied in critical articles and reviews.

ISBN: 978-0-615-27712-7

Library of Congress Control Number: 2009921010

PRINTED IN THE UNITED STATES OF AMERICA

Acknowledgments

First and foremost, I thank God for giving me a vision and blessing me with creativity to write this book, which I hope will have an impact on people's lives. There may be some controversy within these pages, but tomorrow's world is shaped by what we teach our children today. My objective is to educate and entertain my readers. I want to thank my pastor for planting the Word in me on Wednesday nights and on Sunday mornings. I would like to thank my daughter, Ryeshia, for reading the first two chapters and giving me a thumbs up. Your enthusiasm really pushed me to finish this book and I love you very much. I would also like to thank my friend, Wanda Stocks, for being one of my first editors.

Note from the Author

Too often in our communities we forget about our youth who are going through life's journey. *The Age of Innocence* is written through the eyes of two high school teenagers, England and Gabby. They are the main characters, and their lives are filled with responsibilities and difficult challenges. From a teenager's point of view making tough decisions can be difficult, and the challenges can be so intense. Some teenagers go into deep depression when their lives are not what they think they should be. Gabby's and England's parents guided them and mentored them along the way. These girls have high self-esteem, are very active in their church, are athletes, and most of all have a relationship with God. However, they still have to cope with difficult situations that await them on their journey.

The Age of Innocence looks at the behavior of teens and examines their thoughts, fears, and mistakes in building relationships. As preteens move forward into their later teen years, their hormones start to kick in and they begin to experience their sexuality. Some become confused at this stage and start thinking about developing serious sexual relationships without having all the facts. This is the age when teens are starting to pay attention to the opposite sex, and they believe it's time for dating. For some teens, dating is about experimenting, and with experimentation comes emotional highs and lows. Teens need to be guided through these challenging years. Otherwise, they'll make a lot of mistakes that could have been avoided. At this age, building relationships is important to teenagers. They're beginning to learn how to skillfully develop relationships. Although teens think they know it all, they still lack judgment, experience, and wisdom.

England and Gabby have friends from all walks of life. Their journey sheds some light on the HIV and STD epidemics among teenagers as well as adults. For some of their friends, this information may be too little too late. We never thought there would be so many children, adolescents, and teenagers affected by these diseases. They are at the age of innocence. They are at the age where they're supposed to be enjoying school, their friends, and learning how to play several sports, or musical instruments. They are not supposed to be living with diseases that are not curable, but they are. Some contracted these diseases from their parents; others contracted it through risky behaviors. Whatever the case may be, sex education should be a focus and priority for all of us.

Please feel free to contact the author @
bnm1541@charter.net

Chapter 1

England and Gabriel

England Desto and Gabriel McWright (Gabby) were childhood friends. England came from a family of educators, and Gabby came from a family of lawyers. Throughout high school they were cheerleaders, and Gabby also performed with a ballet company. England was the most outspoken child one could ever imagine. She made sure that no one misunderstood her. She was very witty and very dainty. People most often misunderstood her character because she was fastidious. Gabby, on the other hand, was very shy and charming. Both of these girls had a spiritual background because their parents were very active members of great churches in Atlanta. Therefore, the girls knew God and were very aware of His existence. They attended Bible study, church service, and were active in the youth department. You could probably say these girls were well- rounded.

Once the girls entered the eleventh grade, they started applying to colleges. Of course, they wanted to attend the same college. Gabby's parents wanted her to attend an Ivy League school in the field of law, and England's parents wanted her to attend a state university, one they could afford. England knew she wanted to become an educator like her parents, but Gabby didn't want to have anything to do with law. She wanted to also be an educator. But how could Gabby bring this type of news to her parents, especially her father? Well, Gabby didn't do so because she was afraid. Her father had always told everyone that Gabby was going to be a lawyer and take over the firm someday. He had envisioned this dream since Gabby was born. He felt as though she was the smartest of his three children, not to mention the oldest as well, and deserved to run the company.

England was sitting at the dinner table one day when her parents asked about Gabby's plans as a pre-law student. They wanted to know whether she had chosen a school and if the school was located in state or out of state. England had a confused look on her face. She was not sure if she should tell her parents that Gabby was not going to major in pre-law, but in education. Since Gabby's father had told everyone that Gabby was going to major in pre-law, England didn't want to expose Gabby's plan. After a long pause, England's parents looked at her with concern: "What's the matter?"

England said, "Well, uh, you see, Gabby wants to be an educator, not a lawyer."

"What?" said her dad.

"Yes," said England. "She is trying to think of a way to tell her dad. She wants to let him down gently."

"Well, the best thing for her to do is to talk to him and explain why she doesn't want to be a lawyer. I'm sure he'll understand her decision and most of all, I'm sure he will respect her decision. Ultimately, she'll be the one who has to live with her decision. She will have to get up each and every morning and go to her job."

England's mother added, "When you talk with Gabby and she asks you what to do, tell her that she needs to first pray and ask God to give her the words to say to her father, and as she speaks to her father make sure she's speaking words of the Holy Spirit. Truly her father will be upset, but he's a Christian man and will get over it. It's not the end of the world. Sometimes parents have to pull back and let their children make life-long decisions for themselves."

England understood what her parents were saying. They were more readily available to assist her in any way, yet they allowed England to make her own choices. They never tried to tell England what occupation would be best. They just allowed England to explore different jobs and to visit them at work to observe their daily operations. England always enjoyed visiting her mother's fifth grade class. As her mother taught, England would walk around the room assisting students. The children enjoyed the individual help they were receiving. England's father was the principal of a high school and she enjoyed visiting him as well. That afforded her an opportunity to "eye" the boys that were not at her high school. Exploring unfamiliar territory was very exciting.

Gabby's dad, Mr. McWright, had run for judge and won, beating his opponent by 2000 votes. He had one of the largest law firms in Atlanta and was known from coast to coast. Gabby's mother, who was his right hand, was a tough trial lawyer and a partner in the firm. Gabby's mom and dad always talked about cases during dinner, not leaving much time for Gabby to share her teenage experiences with them. Gabby was okay with that when she was much younger because she didn't have much to say. Yet now that she was on her way to college, she had a lot to say but didn't know how to initiate the conversation about her future goals. She knew if it was left up to her father, her goals would be set—the ones that he had set for her.

Gabby knew she had to talk to her parents before responses started coming in from the colleges to which she applied. She knew that she didn't always make it home in time to get the mail out of the box, and it would be tragic if her dad got the mail and started thumbing through it. Gabby contemplated telling her mom since she was affable. Yet Gabby also knew her mom was in agreement with her dad's decision about her future. Gabby finally realized that this might be a little difficult. At that moment, Gabby raised her head and looked toward the sky. Then she closed her eyes as she bowed her head.

Chapter 2

England

England was awakened by her 6:00 a.m. alarm. She didn't want to go to school because it was the big day for final exams before summer vacation. She also knew she was not prepared for her exam in calculus. She had stayed up way past her bedtime watching her videotape of *Days of Our Lives*, taped earlier that day. England made it her business to kneel down and pray in thanksgiving every morning before leaving her bedroom. But this morning she got up with a negative attitude; rushing around because she hit the snooze button and got up much later than she'd anticipated. After taking a shower, putting on her clothes, and doing her hair, she had just a couple of minutes to run out the door before the bus driver pulled up. Glancing in the mirror one more time, England ran out the door and forgot to pray.

The bus started moving before England had a chance to grab a seat. This put her in an even worse mood, and she was angry. She didn't say good morning to anyone, and no one spoke to her. On top of that, she knew she'd forgotten something because she was feeling strange. It didn't dawn on her until she got to school and started walking toward her locker that she had forgotten to pray. She knew that she couldn't start her day without praying. She'd already gotten off to a rough start and she couldn't allow her attitude to get in the way today. She had major tests and needed to be focused. Ken came up to her at her locker and asked what was wrong. England rolled her eyes and said, "What's it to you?"

Ken replied, "Hey, people who ride your bus said you had an attitude problem. You aren't your normal self."

"Well, I overslept and had to rush before the bus came. Now I have to take tests all day."

"England, when you are upset about something you know how we do it. We must pray for God to give us a better attitude. God says that no matter what happens, we should continue to pray. So, what if you didn't have time to kneel at your bedside and pray. God says we can call on him anywhere and anytime. Every place is a praying place. So my advice to you is to go pray and get back on your game before you go to first period. I have to go meet with the guys and I'll talk with you later. I know you'll have an awesome day! You know why? It is the day the Lord has made!"

England knew that Ken was trying to agitate her. He didn't pray, but just got up in the morning and decided which girl was going to be his victim that day. Ken and his best friend Calvin were highly sexually active and to them it was just a game.

As England put her books in her locker, she thought about what Ken had said. She started off to the cafeteria and passed several empty classrooms and a restroom. As she passed the last classroom, she decided to go in. She walked towards the window and stared out; her eyes fixed on a bird that she had never seen at this time of the year. As she stared at the bird, she started to feel a certain presence. She knew that she was in the presence of God, and she was ready to pray and let him assist her in changing her attitude. More than anything, she needed to pass her calculus test. As England prayed, she gave thanks for everything, including the experience she had that morning. She realized she was vulnerable and must stay alert, because Satan was busy and always trying to catch her off guard.

After England prayed, she was more than ready to restart her day. She was ready for her exams, even the calculus exam for which she hadn't studied enough. She felt much better and realized it was not wise to stay up late during final exams, unless she was willing to suffer the consequences. As she reflected on her morning, she also realized that she should always "put on the full armor of God" because Satan would always try to separate her from God. After all, she believed she was a Christian. Knowing this, England understood that Satan's goal was to try to break her down when he thought she was at her lowest.

Chapter 3

Gabby

As Gabby entered the cafeteria searching for England she ran into Ken who gave her his take on England's morning. Gabby was surprised to hear that England had a rough start. She wondered what her night had been like. Gabby was the one who was always late. She was the one who had a car and didn't have to depend on a bus ride to school. However, most of the time she arrived right before the last bell. Since she was early today, she decided to join in prayer with a Christian organization on campus.

Gabby was right on time for the Christian organization's activity. After the opening prayer, the coach posed two questions to the group of young people.

He said, "What time do you usually get up in the morning? When would you like to get up? I want you to think about those two questions as we read Mathew 28:1-20." After the reading of the passage, the students talked about the importance of waking up on time and getting to school on time. Some students said that when they got to school before the first bell rang, they tended to be in a more relaxed state that gave them an opportunity to plan their day. Other students reported that when they got to school late, they didn't have time to meditate or prepare for the day. When they were late, it seemed as though they were then late for every class and meeting, including lunch, and their spirits were just not settled. The discussion ended with the Resurrection of Jesus and concluded with a prayer.

After this meeting, Gabby thought about all the times she was late for class, church, meetings, and sport activities. She asked herself why she was late to so many important events in her life. She felt as though she came to school early just to get this lesson about being tardy all the time. Gabby realized that God had wakened her and gotten her out of the house on time to go to this meeting, which was a wake-up call for her. She could not continue to be late to events. She realized that when she was late, she felt rushed all day. She decided that she needed to make sure to be on time.

This summer was the first time Gabby had a real job. She had to be at work at 8:00 a.m. This would truly be a challenge for Gabby because of her habitual tardiness. Her teachers and friends had always complained about it. Now Gabby had to work hard at changing that negative to a positive. This meeting was not just another meeting. It forced Gabby to take a look at her character. It was the wake-up call that Gabby needed.

Gabby was the first one to class, and she sat and reviewed her notes for the big exam. When England walked through the doorway, she didn't expect to see Gabby. She was absolutely shocked.

"Gabby, girl, this is a surprise! What are you doing here so early? Is everything, okay?"

Gabby said, "Yeah, yeah. I got up early and decided to come on to school. The Lord woke me up on time so I could get to the Christian organization's meeting on time. Guess what the questions were to-day?"

"What?" asked England.

"They were about getting up on time."

"Well, God is definitely moving in this building today," said England. "As you know, I was late this morning and had a bad attitude. I stayed up last night looking at the stories I taped. When my alarm clock went off, I pushed the snooze button. I ended up pushing that button several times and wound up being late. I was not only late, but I also didn't study for the exam like I should have. Ken heard about my attitude this morning, so he came up to me and asked about it. He suggested that I go somewhere and pray before I continued with my day. I was definitely in agreement with him although I knew he was picking on me."

"Yeah, because we know he doesn't pray until he is really caught up in something he can't wiggle out of," replied Gabby.

"Yeah! It's a shame that he and Calvin think so little of themselves. Every year their behavior worsens. They sleep with more and more girls every year. Why is this?"

"England, they are lost, just like a whole lot of teenagers. They think having sex is the going sport right now. They know about sexually transmitted diseases but think it can't happen to them."

"Yes, we all know about that," said England. "It's all over the news. I watched TV yesterday and the reporters were talking about this STD epidemic. The report stated that 25% of girls aged 14 to 19 years old have at least one of the four common diseases, and 50% of those infected are African-American. There are 10 million teenagers infected!"

"My, my, my! Wow! That's a lot of teenagers," said Gabby. "I can't imagine how many people are infected on this campus. A lot of them don't even know they're infected because some diseases don't have obvious symptoms. What about the Human Immunodeficiency Virus (HIV) and Acquired Immune Deficiency Syndrome (AIDS)?"

England and Gabby grew very silent as they thought about Ken and Calvin. They both wondered if one, or both, might have some type of disease.

Chapter 4

Gabby and England

After finishing their exams, they'd agreed to meet Ken and his friends at McDonald's for lunch. Gabby was done first with her exam, so she gathered her things, turned her test in, and went out the door to wait for England. It took England forever to complete her test because she hadn't studied the essay questions. As she pondered her answers, her stomach started growling. She was so hungry she could eat a bear. But she tried not to let her hunger distract her.

In the meantime, Gabby was outside waiting and wondering what was taking England so long. As Gabby's stomach started to growl, she walked to the student parking lot to get her car. She figured that she would pull the car out front so England could jump in. That didn't happen immediately. Gabby had to wait 15 more minutes. As she waited, she listened to *Mary, Mary's* CD and started envisioning her life, wondering where she would be in ten, 20, or even 30 years.

While she was in thought, England appeared on the passenger side, pulling on the door handle, and trying to get in. Gabby unlocked the door and asked her what took her so long. England did not answer; she really ignored the question by starting a conversation about Gabby's career decision. A telephone call interrupted just for a moment. Gabby was getting a call from Ken, who was waiting at Mickey D's with his friends. Actually, they were getting ready to go since Gabby didn't answer his text message. But he decided to call.

"Hello Ken," said Gabby, "we're on our way, stay put."

Ken replied, "You all better hurry because we're tired of waiting."
England started to revisit her thoughts. Gabby hung the phone up.
"Hey, did you tell your dad about your plan yet?" said England.
"Nope!" said Gabby.

As they pulled into the parking lot at McDonald's, they saw Ken,
Michael, and Calvin.

"Oh, my land!" said Gabby. "I can't believe Calvin is with them."

Calvin and Gabby used to date, but Calvin had dropped her and
started dating a girl named Valerie. The girls rushed into Mickey D's
with big smiles on their faces. They sat down and started talking; then
they all decided to place their orders. As they stood in line, Calvin
asked Gabby what was going on in her life and if she'd picked a college to attend. Calvin knew that Gabby's father wanted her to attend
his alma mater. At least, that was what he was told. However, Gabby
didn't know he had this piece of information, so she said she was still
searching. Calvin had already decided on a college in Georgia where
he would be studying pre-med.

After getting their food, they sat down and started talking about
final exams, summer plans, and college applications. Ken was an avid
musician. He played five instruments and read sheet music pretty well.
He was very impressive—going to college on a scholarship. He'd accepted a full band scholarship from the "Marching 100's." England
and Gabby were both preparing to go to school in Georgia. Ken also
mentioned that he'd be working this summer at a band camp for middle school children. This would give him some experience with kids
and music.

Although Calvin was the smartest of them all, he was wild, enjoyed life, and didn't talk much about his ambitions. His mother, who
worked several jobs to pay the bills and keep him looking good, was
raising him. As he sat quietly looking at Gabby, he was wondering
why he'd dumped her in the first place, because the girl he was dating
was just a lunatic. Everything was about her, and nothing was about
him. This attitude did not sit well with him. As he watched Gabby
carefully, he thought about how he'd traded in a godly girl for a de-
mon. He missed being around Gabby and was taking this moment to
observe her in every way. To him Gabby was a ruby— full of holiness.
Now he remembered why he dumped her. He dumped her because she
wasn't ready to give up her virginity and now, he thought that was

11

lame. He still thought she was special and wanted to get back with her, but he knew that she would probably go all off on him if he asked. So, instead he just stared at her.

Ken noticed Calvin staring at Gabby but didn't say a word. England noticed also. Suddenly, all their phones started to ring at the same time. It was their parents checking up on them. Gabby and England had to leave because it was Bible study night. After the girls left, Ken asked Calvin what the staring was all about.

Calvin said, "What are you talking about?"

Ken said, "Whateva, let's go."

Calvin knew exactly what Ken was referring to, but he pretended that he didn't know. Gabby was not someone Calvin wanted to talk about with Ken. Ken thought Calvin was out of his mind when he dumped Gabby for one of the biggest losers in the female department. Also, Calvin knew that Ken would start preaching to him about his behavior toward girls in general. But Ken was actually no saint himself.

Calvin wanted to be a player. Gabby thought he was a player with a game. She always thought that Calvin was walking through life with his eyes closed. He had a lot of book sense but no common sense.

Chapter 5

Gabby

The summer had come and gone and Gabby was approaching her senior year. She'd had a productive summer, having met some interesting young people. Gabby's new friends were Elijah, Sarah, and Matthew. Out of all of them, Matthew was her favorite. His conversations could be so deep. As she thought about an important conversation they once had, she knew it was time to tell her parents that she'd been accepted to Austin State University and wanted to be an educator. Gabby was no longer afraid to discuss her plans with her parents. Matthew had assured her that if she took everything to God in prayer, it would be all right. He also said that God would let her know when the time was right to talk with her parents. The key to knowing when the time was right was the ability to stay focused—to keep her eyes on God. She thought she had done this and that now was the time. She prayed to God to let her father accept the decision she'd made and not get bent out of shape.

It was a Saturday morning two weeks before school. Gabby's mom had been outside all morning when she came in and fixed a late breakfast for the whole family. Her mom turned on the house intercom to call everyone for breakfast.

She said, "Come all who are hungry and ready to eat."

They all came at once. Gabby bounced down the stairs smelling the bacon, her brother and sister came from the game room, and her dad trotted in from his office.

Gabby's mom had the table set so beautifully that morning. Everyone stopped in their tracks and wondered what was going on. Her father thought the table looked great, but he was at a loss for words. He remembered that his mother told him to always show appreciation for the smallest things people did for you. Although the setting of a table was not a big deal, it had to be important to his wife. She took the time to cut roses and other assorted flowers and arrange them in a vase in the center of the table. Furthermore, she used her fancy tablecloth.

Gabby asked, "What's the big occasion?"

"Well," her mom said, "I thought this would be a celebration for you. You'll be our first child to graduate from high school and go on to college. That'll be a great accomplishment and I thought we could start that journey together with you."

Gabby and the rest of the family sat down. Daddy was ready to preach a sermon. Her mom had opened the door and he was going to take advantage.

Her dad said, "Let us pray." He started his prayer by saying, "Heavenly Father, here we are as a complete and whole family. We thank you..."

As her dad prayed, Gabby was thinking about how long he was going to take to pray. Although she always enjoyed her father's prayers, she was a bit anxious to give her news.

"Amen," said her dad.

After the prayer, they began to pass serving plates of food around to each other. After everyone had settled and begun eating, Gabby thought about God first, and then she asked Him quietly if this was the time. The place was appropriately set, and all were in attendance. She didn't hear anything from God. She remained cool and focused. This may not be the perfect time for Gabby, because her brother and sister were present. She didn't know how her father would react, she thought she should tell her parents later behind closed doors.

Everyone was involved in meaningful conversation while Gabby was in her zone. Gabby's brother asked her if she was excited about being a senior.

Gabby responded by saying, "Yes, I'm very excited. This will be an important year for me."

Gabby had a serious look on her face and was in deep thought.

"Why is this a serious year for you?" inquired Gabby's sister.

"Well," Gabby said, "everyone's last year of high school is serious. They have to do their best, practice study skills, and make sure everything is prepared for the next year".

"Speaking about next year, are you ready for the university of our choice? I'm sure you're going to have several instructors that I know," said her dad.

"Well, uh, Dad, I need to talk to you and Mom after breakfast so hold that thought," said Gabby.

Everyone looked at Gabby and then continued to eat. Then the phone rang. It was 9:00 on a Saturday morning so Gabby knew it was grandmother calling from Chesapeake Bay. It appeared that everyone knew because the kids ran to the phone as their parents just smiled.

While Gabby was on the phone, Mom and Dad tried to figure out what Gabby wanted to talk to them about. Her mom had an idea. She remembered Gabby asking her questions about the field of education. Gabby once told her mom that she would be a good teacher. As these thoughts ran through her mind, she was hoping that Gabby's choice was not going to be an issue. If so, she needed to prepare herself now. In order to do this, she had to help get her husband's mind straight because she knew he would possibly be devastated.

So, Gabby's mother said, "Remember that verse from the Bible that says, 'Don't make your children angry by the way you treat them. Rather, bring them up with the discipline and instruction approved by the Lord."

Gabby's father said, "Yes, but you've said I'm getting more mild-mannered, right?"

"Sure, and don't you think we did a good job with Gabby?" asked Gabby's mother.

"Where is this leading?" asked Gabby's dad.

"Whatever Gabby has to tell us, let's try to support her decision, because she must find her own way and might make a few mistakes in order to grow," replied Gabby's mother.

"I don't know what you are talking about, but I don't want her to make mistakes at my expense," said Gabby's dad.

"Dad! Grandmama said come to the phone."

"Coming!"

Gabby waited patiently for her parents in her dad's office. As she waited, she asked God for guidance. She asked Him to give her the words to say. As a young child, Gabby was taught by her grandmother to always take everything to God in prayer. She always reminded Gabby that there would be times when she would need God the most. She thought about the scripture, "Don't let the excitement of youth cause you to forget your Creator. Honor him in your youth before you grow old and no longer enjoy living" (Ecclesiastes 12:1). As Gabby went deeper in her thoughts, she looked back on her days in 10th grade.

She remembered the time she went to a party but had to leave because there was no parental supervision, although the girl's parents had said the party would be supervised. When Gabby got to the party the mom was there, but she left soon after. As soon as she left, the kids went wild, and someone must have spiked the punch because it tasted funny to Gabby. Gabby started thinking back on a lot of incidents and issues. Gabby remembered praying with England when England tried to jump her bike over a board built high on some bricks. She crashed into a parked car breaking her arm trying to do what her other friends were doing. She remembered when Calvin dumped her because she would not have sex. It was at that time that she began believing most kids her age were sexually active. It was also at that time that she felt she'd lost her first boyfriend. It was then that she made up her mind that Calvin was a loser. He had several girlfriends at one time. That was when she realized she hadn't lost anything. It was good that she was strong and disciplined enough to know that keeping her virginity meant everything. At her high school it appeared that everyone was sexually involved. Kids were going home ill, and rumors were circulating about certain people getting Sexually Transmitted Diseases (STDs). It was during this time that she realized God had a purpose for her life.

Now Gabby accepted dates without strings attached. She realized that boys might dump her because of who she was and what she represented. She felt that God had covered her, and she would survive her teenage years. She had vowed to stay true to herself, which seemed hard for other girls. Gabby had a good support system—her parents.

Gabby was in a daze when her parents walked into the office.

Gabby's dad said, "You wanted to see us, young lady?"

He was always so professional and dramatic when speaking to anyone. He had such a baritone voice and she loved to hear him give speeches.

Gabby just came right out and said, "I wanted to let you know that I will be going to ASU to obtain an early childhood degree instead of attending your alma mater, Dad. I know you want me to be a lawyer, but I feel that my calling is education."

Gabby's dad sat down. Quiet filled the room. Gabby's mom was still standing. She looked at Gabby and then at her husband. Gabby continued looking her dad square in the eye. For the first time, Gabby's dad seemed to see her for who she really was. He realized he had raised a young woman who could stand up for herself. He stared at Gabby, overflowing with emotion. He realized he had never really looked at his daughter, I mean *really looked* at his daughter. He was so proud of her. His first-born was taking her life into her own hands and had made an important decision.

Gabby interrupted his thoughts by saying, "Oh yeah! I have a full four-year scholarship! So, Dad, you will not have to pay a penny."

Gabby's dad was even more astonished. He asked, "Well, who helped you fill out the application?"

Gabby said, "England and I completed the applications together."

"So, is England going to ASU also?"

Gabby said yes and that they would be roommates and probably have a lot of classes together. They were both going to major in Early Childhood Development.

The room, once again, became silent.

"Well, Gabby, I don't know whether to be upset or commend you for stepping up to the plate and making a decision about your career. You do know that teachers don't make as much money as lawyers, right? I had wanted you to be a lawyer. I told everyone that you were going to be a lawyer. However, I never asked you what you wanted to be in life. I just assumed, since your mom and I are lawyers that you would follow in our footsteps."

Gabby was excited that her dad had endorsed her decision without a fight. She'd prayed long and hard in the spirit before she gave her parents this news.

Gabby suddenly said, "Well, Dad, my job will be equivalent to yours to some degree. I will be serving people, just like you. The difference is that you will serve them through the judicial system, and I will serve them through the education system. But we will both be fulfilling our dreams and working with people."

Her dad couldn't say a word. He just twirled his cigar around, (which he never smoked). Gabby thought her dad handled this very well. Most of the time he wanted everything to go his way and he was very fastidious. He always wanted to be the one in control. So, she was surprised that he was not pushy at all. Gabby thought maybe her mom had given her dad a heads up on the situation. Well, whatever made him accepting of Gabby's plan was okay with her.

Chapter 6

England

England was reading the newspaper when the doorbell rang.
Her mom yelled, "I'll get it!"

She opened the door and Ken said, "Hello, is England available?"

England's mom called her name and England ran to the door. England's mom told Ken to come in and have a seat. England looked at Ken as if he'd committed a sin.

She said, "Well, Ken, what brings you this way?"

Ken said, "I was just in the neighborhood. I wanted to stop by and say hello to you on this beautiful Saturday."

"So, who were you visiting in the neighborhood?" asked England.

"Mumm, I was just passing through. Don't look at me like that!"

They were both silent.

"Okay, okay, you got me! Well, no one really, I just wanted to stop by and chat with you. What are you and Gabby getting into tonight?"

"Well, nothing much," said England. "What are you and your girl-friend doing tonight?"

Ken responded, "Well, we are having some differences right now. I told her that I was going to a college in Florida, and she thinks that I shouldn't go. I tried to explain to her that I got a scholarship, and I didn't have to pay a dime. She just laughed and asked if I was willing to give up our relationship for some dumb scholarship. I couldn't say a word, so I just walked away."

England saw the sadness in Ken's face but how could she give him a shoulder to lean on when she still had a huge crush on him and was hoping that he would have dumped his girlfriend before their senior year began? She knew she was supposed to say something positive and supportive, but she couldn't say a word. She thought long and hard, but nothing would come out. She turned around and started walking slowly away.

"Ken, she'll come around. Don't think about it. Just think that out of a million applications, yours was one of the chosen. It will be a privilege to march with such a prestigious band that has such distinguished character. You should be excited about starting your new journey. You must remember that you can't run after her and make her change her mind about your going to college in another state. Anyway, she's not the only girl you're dating. You will meet new people, and as people enter your life it may be hard to hold onto a long distance relationship. Sometimes we have to stop and not think, but just listen for God's voice. He will direct our path. Oh yeah! You don't know anything about that, do you?"

England went on, "Sometimes we have to let go of those things and people who tend to hold us back or try to make us feel guilty for wanting all that God has for us. I know letting go is very painful. It is almost like death, especially when you've spent so much time with that one person. You feel like your heart has fallen into your stomach. All you can think about is that person. You think that she would be the one to stand by you out of all the people you know. She should be equally excited about your future. I know when you heard that she'd been accepted to the college of her choice, you were very excited and joyful for her. She should be grateful to have someone like you in her life."

Ken was looking strangely at England. He was saying to himself that the relationship was not that deep. However, Ken was astonished.

He said, "You're a great friend, and I know you'll always be there for me and me for you. But why are you tripping? I go to church too. I listen to the pastor."

"Yeah, you go to church. At least I see you in church. Whether you are listening to the pastor or not remains to be seen. I don't see you exhibiting the behaviors that are being taught in church."

"Well, England, we all can't be like you, all holy and...What's the saying? I knew you when you used to wear pigtails and, now that you're all that, you think you're better than me."

"So, you think I'm all that?"

"Yes, I do."

"Well, I'm glad you know my worth, my brotha! You have been paying attention."

"I have, and I will watch you until you become an old woman with gray hairs under your chin."

They both laughed and England punched him on his arm.

England agreed they had been friends ever since fifth grade. Each year they learned more and more about each other. Ken had had more girlfriends than England had boyfriends. England didn't think it was important to have a boyfriend although she liked Ken. Most boys she knew thought having a girlfriend was all about sex. Still, England was confused about the whole girlfriend-boyfriend dilemma. In her opinion, a relationship of that nature should only consist of conversation, holding hands, a kiss on the cheek, and going on dates. It should not consist of intimate sexual activities. Teens are young and throughout life's journey plenty of people will walk in and out of their lives. They should not be in a rush to engage in grown-up activities because they wouldn't have anything to look forward to once they got married.

Ken told England to give him a call because he wanted to hang out with her or go to the movies. England said she would call him. However, England had no intention of calling Ken. She didn't like to be around him that much because of her feelings for him. She thought that if she were around him a great deal, she would be setting herself up. Ken was not aware that England had a crush on him. Besides, if he knew, they would not be friends. England was very sure about that. In the meantime, Ken was trying to feel England out. He could tell there was a little tension there as he visited with her. He also knew that she was very special to him. He loved England but didn't know what all that entailed. He thought he loved her as a friend or a sister. But he wasn't sure. He just knew that when he needed someone to talk to, she was there to listen to his complaints and issues. To him she was a good friend and a loving person in general.

Chapter 7

Gabby

This was the day that Gabby was supposed to hang out with her new friends, Elijah, Sarah, and Matthew. They had decided to meet for lunch and then go check out a movie. Gabby was lying across her bed reading her Bible before she started her day. This was a ritual for Gabby—she enjoyed spending time with God first thing in the morning. Her meditation always jump-started her day. Just as she was beginning to meditate, she got a phone call from England. She invited England to go with her to meet her new friends that she'd met over the summer. England agreed to go so that she wouldn't think about Ken all day.

After she hung up the phone, she got another call. This time it was Ken on the phone, asking her why they didn't call him last night when they went out. Gabby explained to Ken that they did not go out, although that was the plan. Once Gabby hooked up with England, they got into a deep conversation and never did make it out the door.

Ken asked Gabby, "What was the conversation about?"

"Well..." Gabby said hesitantly, "England posed the question, 'How would you feel if an angel appeared to you with a message about God's plan for your life?'"

There was complete silence.

Then Gabby said, "Hello-o-o!"

Ken said, "I'm here."

Gabby said, "Well, what do you have to say about this?"

"I think that would be kind of scary," said Ken. "Why was that question so deep and why did you take all night to analyze it?"

"Well, first of all, most people would think like you," said Gabby, "that it would be scary, and they would only look at it as a dream and nothing more. They probably would go on with their day and not think about it again. But in reality, the angel didn't come to frighten or terrify you, but to announce God's good news to you. Angels serve as God's agents of instruction, judgment and deliverance."

Gabby was all over Ken and above his head. Ken didn't study the Bible at the same level that Gabby and England did. As a matter of fact, Ken didn't pick up his Bible unless it was Sunday morning when he attended church. He never picked it up throughout the week. Ken wanted to know what inspired Gabby to read the Bible. He noticed how intelligent she was and how she had influenced other people to walk with GOD and believe in His Word. Ken asked Gabby how long she'd been studying the Bible. Gabby told Ken she was introduced to God when she was about eight years old but didn't really start studying the Bible until she was in the seventh grade. She told Ken that if he had God in his life fully, he would not have so many problems with his girlfriends and wouldn't have to burn England's ears with his affairs. Ken was not pleased with what Gabby said.

"So," he replied, "if England didn't want to listen to me complain about my life, she would truly tell me so. Furthermore, you do not have any right telling me not to talk with England about my problems. She is just as much my friend as she is yours. I'm sure when you have a problem, you go to England as well. England is a sensible person who does not take sides. She is the one that we all cherish, because she's smarter than all of us. She speaks her mind and doesn't wait months to tell you, her feelings."

Gabby had thoughts of her own. First, she thought that Ken was a fool and didn't know England that well. Then she thought England had been hiding her feelings for Ken for at least three years now. Therefore, she was not as straightforward as Ken wanted to believe. But it was not Gabby's place to let the cat out of the bag. So, she did not say anything. She just let Ken talk and believe that he knew England better than she did.

Gabby was ready to hang up when Ken asked her what they were doing later that day. Gabby told him they were going out to lunch and to a movie with some new friends that she met over the summer. Ken extended an invitation to himself. He told Gabby he would like to tag along, and Gabby said, "Yeah." She thought it would do him some good to talk to other people who were children of God. Just maybe he would pose a question to the group during lunch. Gabby would not answer but would wait for one of her new friends to answer it. She thought, yeah, this is exactly what he needs; then maybe he'll see the light and stop living in darkness.

This had been a crazy morning for Gabby. All she wanted to do this morning was meditate and read the Word. However, God was using Gabby this morning. It appeared that God wanted Gabby to invite England and Ken to lunch.

Chapter 8

Gabby and Friends

T he restaurant had nice beige marble floors in the foyer and it was decked with white lilies and pink roses. The restaurant had a beautiful décor. Both Ken and England were looking around with astonishment. As they waited to be seated, they admired the stained glasses. Elijah, Sarah, and Matthew walked in, and Gabby introduced them to Ken and England.

They started conversing immediately. Ken, Elijah and Matthew were talking about the basketball game, and the girls were talking about taking more foreign languages. After the maitre d' took them to their seats, they ended the separate group conversations and started another one so they all could participate. Gabby thought it would be a good idea for the others to get more acquainted by talking about themselves. England decided to go first, then Sarah, next Elijah, then Ken, and finally Matthew.

Ken thought Matthew had the most exciting resume of them all. Matthew had visited several countries through a program for students in high school, had lunch with the governor of the state, and attended a black-tie affair with major political players. He had plenty of pictures and recommendation letters to show. He had established himself with high rollers. These connections had landed him plenty of scholarship money. He was ready for college and was very proud of his accomplishments. This was impressive to Ken. Matthew had chosen a road that no one thought of. He wanted to major in theology.

After they ordered their drinks and meals, Ken asked Matthew how he was able to connect with all those important people. So he asked Matthew to elaborate on his accomplishments. Matthew said that his parents did not take advantage of the education that was offered to them for some reason or another. Matthew didn't want to go in depth regarding that situation. As he thought about what his parents told him, he started telling his story. ("Sometimes people can't move forward and away from their mistakes"). Matthew grew up with little, but always had big dreams. He had trained himself to be godly. He knew that godliness had value for all things, holding promise for both the present and the life to come.

Therefore, Matthew had to work hard and strive for his dreams to come true. He told his friends that he began writing down the things he wanted to achieve when he was in the ninth grade, and as he achieved those things, he marked them off the list. He knew that his parents could not and would not be able to send him to any college. He saw himself at the bottom of the crab cage, trying to crawl up the sides to get out on top. He realized that there would be a lot of crabs simultaneously trying to get out, pulling each other down by holding onto a leg or two. So, he had to create a swift plan, one that would not allow anyone to pull him down.

The waiter brought them their food which interrupted Matthew. After everyone was sure they had their food and the condiments to go with it, they blessed the food as a group and started eating. Matthew said he would get back to the story after lunch. They responded together, **"Ohhhhhh!"**

England said, "The man has to eat. He doesn't want to be entertaining us as we eat. He's hungry too."

Gabby replied, "Yeah, you're right."

After taking several bites they all agreed that the food was delicious. Elijah even said that the food was so good that he wouldn't even think about slapping his mama. After they had all tasted each other's meals and were quite satisfied with their service, they sat there waiting on Matthew to continue his story. Ken was very interested in hearing it.

So, Matthew grunted and said, "Okay, where was I?"

Ken started to answer but Matthew said, "Oh yeah!"

As Matthew gathered his thoughts, all eyes became glued on him.

"I was the crab in the bucket—or was it the barrel," stated Matthew.

As Matthew tried to crawl out by using the side of the cage, others were trying to pull him down. Matthew took a route that many did not take. He decided to become a community volunteer. As a community volunteer, Matthew met a lot of people. At a couple of dinners he attended, he was a host and showed people to their seats. Sometimes when he was escorting people to their seats, they would say good evening and start a conversation with him. Before he knew it, they had shared a wealth of information. Sometimes Matthew ran into some of the same people at other functions and he would greet them by name. He said that people like it when you remember them and their names. One time Matthew was supposed to show this couple to their table, yet something was blocking the entrance, so they had to wait. It was really strange at first, and Matthew did not understand until later.

As they waited patiently for the crew to clear the entrance, the madam initiated a conversation that landed Matthew a four-year scholarship. Matthew never talked about his home life with his parents, but for some reason he got into a conversation with this grand lady and started talking. She actually started telling him that she remembered when her husband was his age. They'd been courting when they were in school and her papa was not very pleased, because her husband came from a poor family and her family was wealthy. Her father believed that people should court and marry their own kind. The lady said that you cannot direct your heart. You cannot help who God brings into your life for you to love. Matthew wanted to know how the lady got around her father.

The lady said, "A trustworthy saying that deserves full acceptance is that we have to put our hope in the living God who is the Savior of all men, and especially of those who believe."

She also went on to say, "We are followers of Jesus Christ and we had faith that we could weather any storm and that our love would not die but would live on throughout all generations. And it has done just that."

After hearing this, Matthew started talking about his situation, how he was considered poor and had no money. He didn't think that people would actually talk about being poor. After he shared with Mrs. D and her husband his life story—one that he continued to live—that day began a bright, new adventure for Matthew. He would check the community service board every day to make sure he did not miss any events. Some people at these exclusive events handed Matthew tips, but most of all Matthew was making the connections that he needed to help him get into a major college. Matthew would save his tips so he could buy a better dark suit and nicer shoes to attend these events. Observing how the rich lived was exciting to Matthew. It was even more exciting knowing that some of these people were poor at one time and now had connections. This knowledge helped increase Matthews' self-esteem and build his sense of self-concept. Matthew was one who did not talk much because he didn't want everyone in his business, so to speak. Being a part of the community service council helped uplift him. He was more eager to get out and associate with his peers. He looked forward every day to socialize with students from other schools. Matthew finally had a plan.

At the year end Black-Tie Ball, Matthew saw some people that he had seen at some of the other functions and started talking to them, first by greeting them as he called them by name, then by asking them if they had had a good time as they were leaving. These were his punch lines. He did not have to work hard at it because he was a pleasant gentleman and the older women always complimented him on his manners. They started looking for him and asking the attendants for him by name. Just by being pleasant and courteous, Matthew had touched a lot of hearts.

Everyone enjoyed hearing Matthew discuss his experiences. They could envision Matthew excelling in his plans. After lunch they decided to go to the museum. They walked down the hall viewing the art. As they walked along, Ken thought Matthew was a little too focused and not really enjoying his senior year like most young men their age. Ken really didn't understand that Matthew had to work harder to get where he wanted to go, while Ken's parents were both well-educated and laid the groundwork for him to follow.

Ken was still in thought when they came across the first sculpture of "Madonna and Child." This piece puzzled all of them and they stared at it.

Ken said, "I wonder why they left the dad out of this."

Sarah said, "Maybe the dad wasn't around." Quietness rushed upon them all.

England said, "I wonder what she sees in her child as she looks into his eyes?"

"I think she's praying for the child because she knows we live in a world that is confused and unloving," said Elijah.

"I think she's praying too, asking God to bring out the strength in the child when he has to go through difficulties in life and to help him realize his true potential early on," said England.

"Boy! Some of us still don't know our true potential; we don't even know our calling," stated Sarah.

Ken said, "Speak for yourself," in an angry tone.

"Okay, Ken, what is it that God wants you to do while you're visiting this planet?"

Ken wondered why she had to bring God into this. He had to make up something fast, since England had put him on the spot to look stupid.

He began by saying, "Well, as a young man my age, I know He wants me to receive all the education I can so I can be equipped with the necessary skills to carry out my assignments. Right now, I know the Bible a little and He is going to extend my knowledge on that. I will also be gaining more knowledge in my field of study which is music. As I say this, I'm sure God is going to use me in a powerful way. I will minister through my music."

England was staring at Ken while he spoke, but Ken was not looking in her direction. He knew she would take him down. After he finished, he turned his head slightly to take a glance at England. England turned her head just in time because she had such a smirk on her face. She didn't want Ken to see that she was admiring his acting ability.

The group continued to walk and view sculptures and paintings. Ken could not help but think about England. This would be his last year with England, Gabby, and Calvin. He vowed to make their senior year the best. These were his friends, although England had just challenged him, he held his ground. He enjoyed the challenge. He thought of what he said and realized that he had a job to do, and England really just pointed that out. He looked at England again and thought about how he would always cherish his friends, especially England, because she held a special place in his heart. He did not want to admit this, but it was true. Ken was standing in front of a

Picasso when England walked up on him. She called his name and he almost jumped out of his skin.

England said, "Oh, I'm sorry. I didn't mean to startle you."

Ken said, "That's okay, I was just deep in thought. You put me on the spot, but I came through, huh?"

"Boy, please," said England. "You always think you can wiggle out of situations. Anyway, what were you thinking about?"

"Well, you know we're coming up on our senior year," said Ken.

"Yeah," said England.

"This is it; we're going to go our separate ways and we may never see each other again."

"Stop being so dramatic. Yes, we will! We will see each other over the holidays and during spring and summer breaks. And don't forget that my school will be playing your school in football. I will get an opportunity to see you step with the band."

"And you and Gabby will just be about two hours away," said Ken.

Ken wasn't thinking or talking about the group. He was directing his thoughts to England and England's thoughts were directed to him. They continued to walk, leaving the group behind.

Gabby turned around to say something to England, but England was not in sight. She asked the others where England and Ken went. Everyone looked around wondering the same thing.

"Maybe we left them at the Picasso painting, or they turned down the first aisle," remarked Matthew.

"I don't know," said Sarah.

Elijah said, "They'll catch up with us."

"Yeah, I guess so," said Gabby. "Well, let's go see the French painters. After that I have to go to dance practice."

The group agreed.

"So, what's with your friend, Ken?"

"What do you mean, Elijah?"

"He seems a little edgy."

"Well, Ken is in his own world. He thinks life revolves around him. He's into heavy dating like a lot of people our age, but he's a good person and he —"

"Wow! So, he's probably living a dangerous life right now," interrupted Elijah.

"Yeah, but he knows. We've told him, and our preacher speaks about it on some Sundays."

30

"How do girls look at guys who are still virgins at your school?"

"I really don't know. We hear conversations in the restroom and during lunch about sex. The girls brag on having different sex partners, but they never talk about virgins. They want to claim that everybody is doing it. Why do you ask?" questioned Gabby.

"Well, I am a virgin and guys at my school call me names and they call my friends names," said Elijah.

"That's cruel," said Matthew.

"Yep, but some of those same people are the walking dead," said Gabby. "So, I really feel sorry for them. I feel blessed that God put my focus on other meaningful things for the moment. That doesn't mean that I don't think about it. I just know I'm blessed, and that sex can be a lethal weapon in our time."

Sarah nodded.

"You're right. It's a shame that young people aren't taking responsibility for their actions. Many aren't even thinking about taking an HIV or STD test of any kind," said Matthew.

"That's why it will continue to be passed from one person to another," Gabby added. "No one is asking their partner or partners to be tested before they start their quest."

They all became silent. In the silence, Gabby called England on her cell phone to let her know that they were going to see the French painters and then she had to leave. England told Gabby that if she did not catch up with her, Ken would take her home. Ken nodded his head, agreeing with England.

"Okay, let's go see the French paintings. Then I've got to go."

"Okay, Gabby, let's hurry so you won't be late," said Matthew.

In the meantime, England was shocked that she had made that suggestion and so was Gabby. It was too late to take it back because she didn't want to alarm Ken. Ken was thrilled, but he realized how his stomach becomes queasy when he's alone with England and how his emotions become unsettled. England was thinking how she enjoyed being with Ken. However, she didn't want to let her guard down. She knew that Ken enjoyed dating girls who were like hot tamales, and she happened not to be one of those girls. Therefore, she didn't want to set herself up to be heartbroken by a bad boy. She was trying to play it safe and only be his friend. She wanted to keep her innocence.

Ken, on the other hand, was in denial of his feelings for England.

He always thought of England as smart, intelligent, beautiful, and straight up virgin. He was staring at the floor as he chuckled to himself, entertained by his thoughts. As England turned around to look at him, his head came up and they looked each other straight in the eyes. For that brief moment they both thought they saw something that was real—their feelings were more real than anything. Silence was in the air, and love was also.

England and Ken started talking at the same time. However, they didn't understand what one said to the other. Ken told England to go first.

England said, "Okay! I wanted to know if you would like to go see the Louvre Collection."

Ken said, "Why not? This is the last day for it."

As they started in the direction of the collection, they talked about the upcoming school year and their expectations. As they were in conversation, England saw the preview board that highlighted future museum exhibits. England started to daydream. She thought to herself, "Is this not a love story starring England and Ken, and am I not flying solo? This is crazy! I shouldn't spend time with this boy. He's probably thinking about his date for tonight and is ready to go home, but he just doesn't want to hurt my feelings. After all, I did impose on him."

She turned to Ken.

"Ken, let's hurry up through this one because it's getting late."

Ken looked at her and said, "Late? Oh, do you have a curfew?"

"No! But I know this is the weekend and you probably already have your plans for tonight. I don't want you to be late because of me."

Ken really did not want to let this go. He was enjoying the time with England, although he knew she was not going to let him get too close.

Ken said, "No, I don't have a date tonight. As a matter of fact, I was just going to stay in and do some reading."

Ken really wanted to get closer to England, but he knew that England was aware of his sexual activities in the past. Most of all, he knew England believed that she had nothing to offer him because she was not sexually active. Ken asked himself if this was the time to talk to England, to get into her head and figure out how she was viewing him. England knew Ken was lying about reading because he never stayed home on the weekends. He was either hanging out with his boys, or he had a date with a girl who wouldn't have a problem with his sexual advances.

Ken wanted to initiate a new conversation but was afraid. He was scared that if he opened that door, England would not take him seriously because she knew his track record. He thought about college, girls, parties, God, church, and England—in that order. He knew he liked girls and thought there were going to be plenty in college who were very active and just waiting on him. But he also knew he had to keep his grades up or he would lose his scholarship. And he knew that God was keeping an eye on him because his mom told him so. He had to go to church because everyone in his family were Christians. Then there was England, just like the Virgin Mary. Ken was on a roll with his thoughts. As they walked through the art museum, they ran into Calvin and were surprised to see each other.

Calvin said, "Wow, what are you two doing here?"

Ken said, "We should be asking you that."

They all paused.

"We came with Gabby and her friends from her summer job, and you?"

Calvin said, "I brought Nikki to view the collection of Louvre."

"Oh, did you now?" said England.

England and Ken both were thinking the same thing. They knew that Calvin was up to no good, because although he had good grades, art was not his thing.

Calvin said, "Nikki, meet England and Ken, my friends."

They greeted Nikki with a smile and told her it was good to meet her. Calvin was looking very uncomfortable, wondering why Ken was with England, especially when he knew he could not have his way with her. He wondered if Ken had wandered off the beaten path.

After they chatted for a minute, Ken and England decided to view the Louvre collection swiftly and then leave. Ken already knew he had to explain to Calvin why he was with England. How could he explain something that he really didn't understand himself? Calvin always lusted after girls, always fantasizing about having sex with them. Ken had his first sexual experience when he was about ten years old. He was searching through his dad's toolbox looking for a wrench to fix his bike, when he came across his dad's magazines. He viewed his dad's magazines on a regular basis without his dad knowing about it.

At that early age lust was aroused in him. The more he viewed the magazines, the more he fell into bondage. As he entered middle school, he viewed girls as sex objects. Lust had become a way of life for him.

On the way home Ken was very quiet. He tried to come up with reasons for why he enjoyed England and respected her so much. He knew he himself was a person who had committed great sins, but he always allowed his sexual temptations to overpower his ability to do the right thing. He always dated girls just so he could have sex with them. His thoughts about them did not go beyond that. For Ken, sex was just a part of dating, a casual thing for him and some of his buddies. They did not look at sex as immoral because they got enjoyment and temporary satisfaction out of lusting. For Ken, this seemed normal for guys his age and there was nothing wrong with it in his eyes.

Ken and England arrived at England's home a little past six. Being his normal charming self, Ken got out and opened the door for England. England invited Ken to come inside her home, but Ken said he must be on his way because he'd been gone all day and his mom had already called once. They both said goodbye and Ken got in the car and drove away. England was exhausted, but not exhausted enough to head upstairs to her room. She went in the kitchen to find her parents at the table eating.

Her mom said, "Well, good evening, young lady. Did you have a good time with your friends?"

England said, "Yes."

Her mom expected more than that because normally England would freely share details of her outings with her friends. But, for some reason, England appeared to be preoccupied.

Her dad replied, "Well, honey, how did you get home?"

England said, "I got a ride home with Ken because Gabby had to leave early to go to dance practice."

"Well, how is Ken? I haven't seen him lately," said her dad.

"Well Dad, you know Ken," England paused. "Ken is Ken, doing the same things he has been doing since the beginning of high school."

"And what's that?" asked her dad.

"Being a jerk!" England exclaimed. "He just doesn't get it, Dad. He goes around dating girls just to have sex with them, and some of them are fools because they allow him to smooth talk them into doing it. Then he acts as if sex is supposed to be a part of dating."

England's dad said, "England, let's talk. Come and sit with me a while."

England's dad told her that because kids lack parental guidance, some boys and girls think that sex is dating.

"These are the things that they see on TV and hear in their music," he said. "TV shows and music have a lot to do with how people react to certain subjects. They try to emulate what they see on TV or hear in music, not realizing that this is just an act, just entertainment. It is not meant for people to take these acts and incorporate them into their lives. It would be good if TV had more positive shows and more shows related to biblical values. People watch more TV and listen to more radio shows than anything else. We live in a confused world, one that has a different agenda from God's agenda. We must continue to stay prayed up. We are always going to be looked upon as outcasts because we are trying to live right, while others are exposing themselves to Satanic activities, they call fun."

As England's dad looked at her, he realized that he and his wife had done an excellent job raising England. He was proud of England. He knew that she and her friends were at the age of innocence. He realized that the teenagers faced a lot of peer pressure, and it took a strong person with values and morals to survive in this world today—and this world was not getting any better. To begin with, people were taking other people's lives as if it were nothing. Children were committing adult acts without knowing the consequences. This world was full of pain—pain that men had inflicted upon themselves. We, as a people, he thought, could destroy this world. We were dying each and every day, yet we walked around here as if nothing was going on.

England noticed that her dad was in another world. As he stared out the window, she asked, "Dad, what are you staring at?"

He blurted, "Age of Innocence? Nothing, I was just thinking."

"What are you thinking about, Dad?"

"I was thinking that you need to make sure Ken speaks with the youth minister on Wednesday. He needs some guidance in his life. I just may have to speak with him myself," said England's dad.

"No!" said England. "He would know that I've been talking to you about him, and then he would never tell me anything else. Anyway, he goes to church and the pastor has touched on the subject many times.

We need to find a way to communicate with him without making him feel betrayed."

"All right, all right!" said England's dad. "But are you aware that most of the children, adolescents, and teens treated for HIV are African American?"

"That's a lot of kids! I'll just have to persuade him to talk with the youth counselor," said England.

England's dad was wondering how she was going to persuade Ken to talk to the counselor since he was such a knucklehead.

"What about his dad, England?"

"Well, if his dad was doing such a great job, Ken probably would not be this way. Besides, his dad is always working."

"That's not good."

They were silent for a moment.

"Well," said England's father, "we'll come up with something."

Chapter 9

Gabby and England

This was the first day of school and kids were all over the place. The freshmen were in the wrong halls, and schedules were all messed up. People were angry and upset because they didn't get the classes they signed up for during registration. The line outside the counselor's office was long. Gabby and England knew this was going to be a long day.

"What up, Gabby and Land?" someone yelled out.

Gabby and England turned around and it was none other than Ken.

"Hi," they both said in unison.

"Well, is this a mad house or what?" asked Ken.

"Yeah, tell me 'bout it," said England.

As they walked through the crowded hallways trying to get to their classes, they ran into Calvin. It was like he was running for cover.

"Boy, what is this?" asked Calvin. "Why do we have so many people in our hallways?"

"Well, we gathered that some freshmen can't read their schedules, or they came over here to take a look at the senior meat that was being displayed," said England.

Calvin and Ken looked at each other and started distancing themselves from the girls. Gabby looked at them and said, "You'll need to go sit down somewhere, because you're too old and too spoiled. You've been giving yourself to girls for over a century."

Then the girls started laughing. However, it was not so funny to

Calvin and Ken. Calvin looked at Gabby and wanted to attack her virginity. But he didn't. It wasn't that serious what they said. In fact, it was true with just a little bit of exaggeration.

Calvin looked at Ken and Ken said, "What?"

After getting through the maze of the kids in the hallways, they finally reached their destination. Gabby and England entered the room, then Calvin and Ken. The girls turned around to wave bye, with a big, silly expression on their faces.

Gabby asked, "Where are you all going?"

Ken said, "To class."

"You're kidding me, right?" said England.

"No, we're not," said Calvin.

The girls were stunned, and Gabby wanted to say "sh-t" but only thought about it. The girls rechecked their schedules and snatched the boys' schedules out of their hands to make sure they weren't being facetious.

Calvin said, "Girl, what is wrong with you?"

"I am just making sure you're in the right class," said Gabby. "And you are!"

England shook her head in surprise. This was going to be an interesting semester. It would probably be very uncomfortable for the four of them, ex-boyfriends, ex-girlfriends, and friends who have crushes on each other. Would this be a bumpy ride?

Gabby, England, Ken, and Calvin took their seats and waited for the teacher to summon the class to order. Right before the teacher closed the door, none other than China ran through the doorway.

Yeah! This was really going to be a roller coaster ride. Calvin had his ex-girlfriend and the new girlfriend in the same class with him. Can it get any more exciting than this England thought? As England looked at China, China stared back. England could not help but remember the day when China tried out for cheerleading. It was not a good day for China. She had forgotten the dance routine as well as the words to the cheer. She was so focused on the judges that she intimidated herself. England and Gabby were embarrassed for her. They tried to help her out, but she wouldn't make any eye contact with them. As a matter of fact, she was sure they were in the stands laughing at her. She also believed that Gabby was jealous of her because she was dating Calvin. Yes, China knew that Gabby used to be one of the girl-friends. Gabby was one of the most popular girls in school because of her charm, beauty, intellect, and God-fearing ways. China didn't understand it. She thought a girl should be popular if she had a boyfriend and she found opportunities to flirt with other boys, among other things.

Weeks went by and the girls ignored the fact that China was in their class along with Calvin and Ken. The boys had been discussing Nikki as they approached the class. Calvin had told Ken about his plans to dump China. Calvin thought China flirted too much and he was getting these weird phone calls from girls, as well as guys, about China. As they entered the room, China beckoned for Calvin to come sit by her. Calvin did just that, while Ken grabbed a seat closer to the front of the room.

This week was Homecoming, and all the students were excited about the game and not too concerned about their academics. Every day had its own theme. The girls were discussing their plans for the party after the game.

Chapter 10

Gabby and England

G abby and England were preparing for the Homecoming game when the doorbell rang. England went to answer the door. She was surprised to see Ken at the door. England was wondering why he was there. Why didn't he get a date for this weekend?

"What's up?" said Ken.

"Nothing," said England.

"Well, I decided to stop by to see if you'll need a lift to the game."

"Boy, you know I don't need no lift. Gabby is upstairs and we're riding together. Why aren't you hanging with Calvin?"

"Well, Calvin is going to the game with China and her friends, and I decided not to swing their way," said Ken.

"So, why don't you have a date? It isn't like you to not hang out with a girl, and it's homecoming too!"

"England, are you going to let me in or are you going to continue with your drill?"

"Oh yeah! Come on in," said England. "So, you want to hang out with us tonight, huh!"

"Yes, but if you girls have dates," said Ken, "then I'll go solo to the game."

Ken knew that they didn't have dates because they couldn't stand the boys in their senior class. He was looking at himself as their date."

"No dates! But we're going to meet up with Sarah, Elijah, and Matthew later. So, if you're taking us to the game, then you'll have to hang with us the rest of the evening."

"I don't foresee a problem," stated Ken.

"Okay! Have a seat and we'll be ready in about ten more minutes," said England.

England ran back upstairs with a big smile on her face to tell Gabby about the plan. Gabby was surprised that he popped up, but she was not surprised that he wanted to be around England. Gabby knew that Ken really enjoyed being around her. Gabby believed that it was a serious crush, and neither one would admit that they were attracted to each other. It went beyond friendship.

"Hurry up, Gabby! We don't need to be late," said England.

As England continued to pack her cheerleading bag with extra clothes, Gabby observed the look on England's face and thought this was an opportune time to mention something about her obvious crush on Ken.

Gabby said, "You know, I haven't seen Ken with any girls lately. Have you?"

"Come to think of it, I haven't. Well, I really haven't been paying that much attention."

"So, I see. What do you think is going on?" Gabby asked.

"Well, maybe he's just maturing—realizing this is the age of innocence and sex is not included," said England. "Or he could be taking a break from the dating scene, or really hoping that the last girlfriend will come back with an understanding."

"Do you want to know what I think!" said Gabby.

"Shhh," said England, "not so loud. And what's that?"

"I think he has his eyes on you, and I also think you like him just the same."

England thought about it and just laughed a little.

"Let's go!" said England. "You are truly tripping."

"Whatever!" said Gabby.

As they walked down the stairs, England was a bit perturbed because Gabby was reading her so well. England thought of telling Ken about how she felt, but knew Ken only dated girls who were sexually active, and she did not want to make a fool out of herself. There were times when England questioned her parents' beliefs. Her parents had made sure that England knew the consequences of having sex at an early age. They made sure she knew she was at the age of innocence.

They introduced her to the Bible, rented videos on teenage pregnancy, and took her to talk with a counselor on abstinence. England just knew that she could never have a real boyfriend because the word "boyfriend" itself was loaded with sexual connotations. The girls at her school were always talking about their boyfriends and how they spent a lot of their time on the telephone. What England did not understand was how everyone knew the routine or formality of the dating scene. If you dated your boyfriend for about two months and you were not having sex with him, he moved on. Or if you dated your boyfriend for about six months and had sex with him all the time, then it was time for him to look for new prey. Either way, he still moved on. The general outcome of both scenarios was that the jerk fled to greener pastures.

As the girls reached the bottom of the stairs, Ken rose from his chair.

"It's about time! That was the longest ten minutes of my life."

Gabby said, "Well, hello to you, too!"

"Oh, hello, Gabby. And how are you doing today?" said Ken.

"I'm doing just fine. How's your mother?"

"She's in much better health these days," stated Ken.

"Well, now that you have all that out of the way, let's ride," said England.

Ken popped the trunk of the car and put the girls' athletic bags inside near his instrument. They waited for Ken to open the doors and help them into the car. They both liked that part about Ken. Ken's parents had raised him well. However, England thought, they didn't do well with the conversation about sex and sexually transmitted diseases.

After Ken got in and started driving, Gabby posed a question. She asked what happened to the girlfriend he had before school started. Ken looked at England, who was seated in the front passenger seat. Then he said, "Well, we decided that the relationship was not working."

"Why wasn't it working," asked Gabby.

"She didn't like the fact that I'm going to college in Florida. She thought it was a dumb idea. So, I thought it would be best to let the relationship go now rather than wait until later."

"Well, where is she going to school?" asked England.

"I don't know. That's not important to me right now," said Ken, trying to get off the subject.

"Well, Ken, you will be close to us. Our schools are probably about an hour and thirty minutes away from each other--no more than two hours," said Gabby.

"Yes, England and I talked about that. I could probably come to visit you ladies during off season," said Ken.

"What do you think about that, England?" asked Gabby.

"Well, I don't think anything. I'm assuming that we all will be so busy that we won't have time to visit each other," said England.

"What do you mean by 'we'? We, as in you and me, are going to be in the same room! We won't have to visit each other," said Gabby.

England felt as though Gabby was trying to get something started. Ken was wondering if England had been talking to Gabby about him, because he thought Gabby was looking too far into the future. It appeared that she knew something. England thought that Ken would go to college and get wild with all the fine ladies that would be coming in from all over the world. Ken thought that England would probably get a boyfriend when she got to college. She would be running into some aggressive upperclassmen who would make her head swing two times. Someone would put a charm on her that her daddy couldn't imagine. Ken's thoughts were making him very upset. Although he liked England, he knew that England would never sleep with him. But, at this point, Ken just enjoyed being around England, enjoying her sweet smell and sweeter smile. She was very beautiful, and he just didn't know what was keeping her from him.

As they pulled into the school parking lot, they could see the band, the cheerleaders, and the buses from the visiting school. After Ken opened the doors, the girls jumped out and looked around. As they stared at the people entering the grounds of the school, someone yelled out England's name from one of the visiting buses. England waved and smiled.

"Who is that?" Gabby asked.

"That's John," said England.

"John. Do I know this John?" Gabby asked.

"No, I don't believe, but I introduced him to you. He's the son of my mom's co-worker."

Ken also wanted to know who this boy was. He was trying to overhear what the girls were saying as he pulled their cheerleading bags out of the trunk. After giving them their bags, he went back to the trunk

BARBARA MURRELL, ED. D.

to get his instrument. Before he could close the trunk, he caught a glimpse of the boy. The boy was giving England a big hug. He hurried to close the trunk so he could be introduced to him. As he came upon them, England was introducing him to Gabby.

"Oh, yeah!" England said. "This is Ken."

The boy held out his hand and said, "Hello, I'm John." The boys shook hands.

"It's a pleasure to meet you," said Ken.

After John ended the conversation, he told England he would see her later. Ken was thinking What did he mean, see her later? He won't be seeing her anytime soon, thought Ken, because he would be present wherever she went tonight.

"Well, girls, I have to go and line up for the march in. I will talk to y'all during half-time," said Ken.

"See ya!" the girls said.

"Well," said Gabby, "let's go so we'll have time to warm up before we have to go onto the field."

As the girls walked down to the field, they were talking about what Ken meant when he said he didn't want to hang out with Calvin that night because Calvin was hanging with China and her friends. They started to give it a little more thought and analyzed the situation.

What do you think about that?"

"You know, Gabby, Calvin was with this girl at the museum named Nikki or Nicole before we started school. So maybe Ken does not want to be involved in a bad ending. China claims to be Calvin's girlfriend, but I don't know because he was holding Nikki's hand at the museum."

"I noticed when we started school Calvin was kind of tense," England continued, "because China was in the same class with all of us. He looked a little flushed on that first day. At first, I thought maybe he was uncomfortable because he used to date you, then I started thinking back to when we met Nikki. He was fidgety then."

"So just maybe he thought you and Ken had figured out that he was still up to his game, dating multiple girls at one time," said Gabby.

Without hesitation, England replied, "He didn't have to think about Ken because he knows Ken is going to have his back, as he too plays the cheating game. Therefore, Ken knows the deal. Furthermore, Ken

44

probably already knew about Nikki. He was just putting on a front for me."

"I get your point," said Gabby.

As the girls entered the circle with the rest of the cheerleaders they saw Calvin, China, and her friends entering the gates of the football field. Calvin waved at them, and then China waved. They waved back with smiles on their faces. China had her head up so high; she could have been the Queen of Scotland walking beside her King.

However, there was no great smile on Calvin's face. As a matter of fact, he looked sick. He looked as if he wanted to be somewhere else, with someone else. Gabby thought China may have demanded that Calvin take her to the homecoming game since they'd been dating for several months. Maybe she threatened to stop satisfying his manly needs if he refused to be seen with her at one of their senior events. Well, whatever the case, thought Gabby, he was with her tonight whether he wanted to be or not.

The girls headed to the football field. On their way they saw Matthew, Sarah, and Elijah whom they invited to the homecoming game. They were delighted to accept the invitation because they didn't have many friends at their school and their peers thought they were just overly intelligent geeks who knew the Bible extremely well.

Elijah called out to Gabby and England and waved fiercely at them. The girls waved back and told them to meet at the track gate so they could talk for a minute. They nodded their heads in agreement.

The girls were going to cheer on the tracks, so they dropped their bags and headed towards the gates to meet their friends. After reaching the meeting place, they exchanged greetings again.

"Matthew! Boy, do you have on some nice threads tonight," yelled England.

"I must agree," said Matthew, grinning.

"Who is the special girl?" England said jokingly.

"It just might be you," Matthew said. "It depends on how well you cheer tonight."

They all laughed at the way Matthew was acting, as if he was Mack Daddy himself. Gabby told them to meet after the game at the same gate where they came in. She also told them that Ken was going with them tonight. They agreed and decided to find the best seats in the house.

As Gabby and England headed back to the field, England spotted Nikki. At least she thought the girl was Nikki. But why would Nikki be here? Nikki didn't attend their school, thought England, and surely Calvin did not invite her. England stopped and continued to watch the girl as she came closer. Gabby yelled at England to come on, but England told her to go on and she would catch up later. England started walking toward the girl, and England realized that the girl was indeed Nikki.

England stood at the gate. waiting for Nikki to get a little closer so she would not have to yell as loud. Once the girl got closer, she yelled her name and Nikki looked her way. Nikki was clueless and she had a silly look on her face as if to say, "Do I know you?" Nikki started walking closer to the gate to get to England.

"Hello, Nikki, do you remember me--England, from the museum? Calvin introduced us."

"Oh, yes!" Nikki said with a giggle.

"Well, I am surprised to see you here. Don't you attend an academy across town?"

"I do, but I decided to surprise Calvin and come to his homecoming game."

This is going to be a hot mess, England thought. How could she stop this from happening? Nikki was going to get embarrassed by China who has no class but loves attention.

"By the way, have you seen Calvin?" asked Nikki.

Do I really have to answer that question honestly? Thought England. As England started to answer, Gabby came up behind her and said "boo" in her ear. England screamed so loud the people thought something was wrong with her. England turned around and yelled at Gabby.

"What's wrong with you?" said Gabby.

"You scared the freakin' mess out of me, girl," England said, trying to remain calm.

"Hello, my name is Gabby."

"My name is Nikki."

"This is Nikki who was at the museum with Calvin that day we all decided to go after lunch," said England.

England tried to make sure that Gabby got the picture without asking questions.

The cheerleader coach was yelling for the girls to come onto the field before the football players arrived. England thought this was a wonderful time to exit and be saved.

Gabby and England said in unison, "Bye Nikki and have fun."

Nikki said, "Bye and I'll talk to you girls later."

England and Gabby both looked at each other. England shook her head and Gabby said, "This is definitely going to be a sick mess."

"Yeah, I was trying to think of a way to help her. She is here by herself, and China and those coyotes are going to eat her alive."

"Well, I pray God will help her tonight," said Gabby.

The cheerleaders were holding the banner for the boys to tear through, and Gabby and England ran down the field to help. After the introduction of the football teams and coaches, the girls yelled and performed flips all the way back to the tracks where they would be cheering. England tried to get Ken's attention, but he was busy playing his horn. So she called Elijah to the gate. She told Elijah to get Ken's attention and tell him that Nikki was here.

Elijah did just that. He walked up through the crowd and the band and waited for Ken to stop playing his horn. Once Ken stopped, one of the band members tapped him on the shoulder and pointed his finger toward Elijah. Elijah tried to yell out the information, but Ken did not understand what he was saying. So, Ken started walking toward Elijah, but his band director told him he knew the rules and could not leave the stands until it was time for the half-time show. After Elijah realized that Ken was not going to be able to come to him, he decided he would go to Ken. Elijah felt desperate to tell Ken what England had said. He noticed the unstable look on England's face. As he made his way through, people were shoving and pushing him.

"Boy, these people are feisty!" Elijah exclaimed.

"You should not be in this section. Anyway, what's the problem?" asked Ken.

"England wanted me to tell you that some girl named Nikki is here," shouted Elijah.

"What! Why is she here?" asked Ken.

"I don't know," said Elijah.

"I didn't mean for you to answer that. I know you don't know. As a matter of fact, you don't know her," responded Ken. "But this is going to be seriously ugly unless we can stop it."

"Stop what!" Elijah asked.

"Okay, give me some time to think. Tell England I got the message, and I don't know if I can stop anything due to the position that I'm in right now. But I'll try. Also, tell her to look up at me throughout the evening and we'll get some signs going on."

Elijah agreed to tell England what Ken had said, but he was also anxious to know what was going on. After Elijah delivered the message to England, England nodded in agreement. Then Elijah went back to his seat.

The cheerleaders were cheering, and the band was playing "Lean with Me, Rock with Me" when the commotion started. Nikki saw Calvin standing near the concession stand as if he was waiting for someone. She came up behind him and covered his eyes.

"Guess who?" said Nikki.

"Hmm… I don't know," said Calvin.

"I'm your surprise tonight," said Nikki.

China was in line at the concession stand when she turned around trying to spot Calvin. She saw Nikki with her hands over Calvin's eyes. She did not know Nikki, but she knew it was a slim girl decked out in a brown Armani pin-striped pantsuit with a Gucci shoulder bag. At the same time, Ken was dancing with his horn and, turning in that direction, saw Nikki and Calvin. He stopped abruptly and looked around. He was looking for China. His heart started beating faster because of what he feared was getting ready to go down. Ken tried to summon England, but England was into her cheer and was not paying attention.

Calvin recognized the voice, but he thought he was dreaming because he could not imagine that Nikki would drive across town without telling him. He also knew he was in hot water because China was close by. He began stuttering, his heart beating fast. He finally yelled out "Nikki!" Nikki released her hands from around his eyes and started laughing.

"Yeah!" Nikki exclaimed.

Calvin turned around and Nikki planted a kiss right on his lips and gave him a big hug while Calvin hugged her back only slightly. China saw all of this in full view and her mouth flew open in anguish. She got out of line and walked quickly toward them. Ken spotted China and asked the band director if he could go to the restroom. Normally, this was not allowed; but Ken pleaded with the director, saying it was an emergency. The director knew he could not legally deny a student a bathroom break, so he gave him permission to go. Ken leaped from the stands and ran towards Calvin and Nikki. He got to them before China. Rudely butting in, he tried to make Nikki give him the attention by hugging her.

"Hi, Nikki, how's it going?" asked Ken.

"Well, hey you," said Nikki.

Ken gave Nikki a long hug simultaneously looking in Calvin's direction.

"England told me to bring you to her if I saw you again, and whatta you know, here you are!"

As Ken grabbed Nikki's hand, China stopped them in their tracks.

"Hold up!" ordered China.

They all looked around at China. Except for Nikki, their mouths were open. China looked Nikki in the eyes and proceeded to claim her man.

"My name is China and I want to know who you are and why you were all over my man!"

Ken interrupted, "You don't have to answer that! Let's go."

"Hold up, hold up!" shouted Nikki.

Nikki thought China was talking about Ken.

"Bring that to me one more time!" exclaimed Nikki.

"B-tch, you heard me, I didn't stutter!"

"All right, China, it doesn't call for all of this!" shouted Calvin.

"Ken is not my boyfriend. I was just giving him a hug."

"Ken! I am not talking about Ken; I'm talking about Calvin!"

"What!" cried Nikki. "Calvin, what the hell is going on? Are you cheating on me?"

China chuckled and yelled "CHEATING!"

China rolled her eyes, looked at Ken, and punched him in the face. Then she turned around and tried to slap Nikki in her face, but Nikki blocked it and punched China on the side of her face. Calvin tried to hold Nikki. At that moment China went wild and Nikki tore away from Calvin. They were fighting like two grown men.

People started running towards the fight. China's girlfriends were trying to get in closer to help China out, but the crowd would not let them. Everyone knew that they would jump a girl and leave her for dead. This was a gang of girls who did not fight fair. However, this was the first time China was actually fighting one-on-one with no help. Her friends got mad and started hitting the people who would not let them by, and the people started hitting them back. Before you knew it, there was one huge fight. Everybody started fighting. The people who did not like China and her comrades jumped into the fight. Although Nikki was getting the best of China, it didn't stop China's enemies from getting some licks in.

Police came running from both sides of the tracks. There were more people involved than the few police could handle. The cheerleading coaches, band director, and some football coaches ran towards the fight to assist the officers. Ken was trying to pull Nikki off of China. He was yelling in her ear, "Let's go before you get suspended from school!" While other students were fighting and punching on China, Ken grabbed Nikki's hand and cut them out a path through the crowd. As he was getting hit, he managed to guide Nikki under the bleachers where the band was seated.

Nikki yelled out in exhaustion, "I don't have my shoes or my purse!"

"Okay, stay here!" Ken cried. "Don't move! I'm going to try to find them! Don't move!"

England saw the fight break out and knew it was China and Nikki. She was looking up into the stands for Ken. She noticed that Ken was not in his place, so she figured he was down on the grounds trying to render some assistance. She jumped over the fence and ran beneath the nearest set of bleachers. She ran in the direction of the fight until she reached Nikki.

Nikki, are you okay?" asked England.

"Yes, I am," insisted Nikki.

"Where is Ken?"

"He went back to find my purse and shoes," responded Nikki.

"Oh, my God! I hope his director can't spot him, because he will definitely be suspended from the band and will risk losing his scholarship," said England.

Nikki started crying, saying that this was her fault and that she never should have come to the homecoming. England tried to console her but the only thing that England could think about was Ken— if his band director spotted him, he would be in big trouble.

"No, this is Calvin's fault. He never should have tried to date several girls at one time."

Ken returned with the purse and one shoe. He told the girls that he had to get back in the stands before someone noticed him missing in action. England told him to go ahead, and she would make sure that Nikki got out safely.

"Well, girl, let's see if you can do a disappearing act," said England. "I know the lady at the back gate over there. If you can get out without being noticed, you won't have to do time at the police station tonight. Let's hurry."

England walked quickly with Nikki to the back gate. She gave Nikki her cell phone number and told Nikki to call her once she got in her car and locked the doors. Once they reached the gate, England explained to the ladies that Nikki needed a quick escape because she was trying to defend herself against China and a big fight broke out. The ladies were not surprised. Everyone knew China and her fighting friends.

"Girl, did you get you some good licks in?" asked one lady.

"Yes ma'am," said Nikki.

Nikki squeezed through the gate and took off running toward her car. England's eyes followed Nikki until Nikki disappeared into the night. Nikki promised she would call England's cell phone and leave a message once she got safely in her car. As England was walking back to the track, she thought about how fast Nikki was running. For Nikki to be Miss Ivy League, she could run pretty fast. England did not know that Nikki was a long distance runner and that scouts were looking at her from top universities all over the country. She was also a martial artist who knew how to block kicks and punches at a fierce speed.

After Nikki got into her car safely, she called England, left a message, then started out of the parking lot. As she drove, she thought about the incident. She thought about how Calvin had told her that she was the only one. He told her that he loved her. She remembered saying "no" to Calvin when Calvin asked her to have sex with him. He was in agreement and assured her that it was okay if she was not ready. During those months when she kept her innocence, Calvin was always on point and on time. Nikki thought he was the most important person in her life. He did not pressure her.

The story changed after sex became part of the relationship.

Nikki shouted, "How long? How long have I been getting played?"

She thought of all the times he came up with excuses for being late or didn't show up at all for their dates. He told convincing lies. Nikki thought how stupid she'd been to believe everything he told her. As she thought about this, tears rolled from her eyes. She felt so empty and so alone. She could not believe that she'd gotten so involved with Calvin that she forgot to take care of herself. She did not rely on her gut feelings, nor did she practice the teachings of her mother. She was so embarrassed she could only cry about her mistakes, as she analyzed her decisions regarding her relationship with Calvin.

She was blown away. She couldn't forget how she had become so relaxed with Calvin and let her guard down, allowing him to step into her dreams. She was trying hard to recollect and figure out where she went wrong and how this had affected her mental state.

Chapter 11

England

England was awakened by the loud sound of a lawn mower. It was about 9:00 a.m. England pulled the covers over her head. She was exhausted from last night's activities. She lay in her bed reflecting back on it all. She could not believe how Calvin could be so self-centered. How could a person go around using people to fulfill his fantasies? How could a person be so heartless? All of this was such an eye-opener for England. She thought she was missing something years ago when girls would talk about how they were having sex and how it made them feel like a woman.

Now she knew having sex does not make you a woman, having sex does not make you mature, having sex does not make you a better person, and having sex only makes you become attached to that person who will leave you sooner or later. More than anything, having sex can give you incurable diseases. At this young age, England knew that a boy could not be committed to one girl—much less to two. Some thought it was in a boy's make-up to get as much sex as he could from more than one partner. It was hardly likely they would love you at such a young age—they were experimenting and just going with their hormones. She often thought about what sex would be like with Ken. Was that lust? She dared not mention these thoughts to Gabby. Gabby would definitely throw the Bible at her.

In the middle of her thoughts, the telephone rang. She looked at the caller ID and saw that it was Nikki. She jumped up and grabbed the phone.

"Hello!"

"Hi, England, this is Nikki. Is it too early?"

"Oh no!" cried England. "I'm glad you called."

"Well, I just wanted to thank you for helping me out last night," Nikki said. "I don't know how to repay you. I shouldn't have shown up at your homecoming unannounced. I know I put a damper on things, and I apologize for spoiling your night."

"Nikki, Nikki, don't you worry about that!" exclaimed England. "I'm just glad that you were not hurt! China is a person who never fights fair! She and her friends always double team girls. I'm glad that you got out of there safely. I really thought I might have to help you fight. I'd been trying to figure out how to talk to you about Calvin. Now that you saw him in action, I don't have to tell you about him; what is next for you?"

As Nikki prepared to answer England, the other phone line rang, and England told Nikki to hold on as she picked up the other call.

"Hi, Gabby, what's up?"

"Nothin' much. Ken said he was trying to call you, but there was no answer."

"Well, I didn't hear the other line buzz. Anyway, I have Nikki on the other end, and I'll call you back."

"Wait, don't hang up yet! Ken wants to meet us for lunch. He said he has something to tell us and it's very important. Can you meet?"

"Yes, I'll call you and get the details when I finish talking to Nikki."

"Okay, bye."

"Hey, Nikki, sorry to keep you waiting. Now what were we saying?"

"Well, you were asking me what was next."

"Yes, are you planning to continue to date Calvin? You know he's going to back this entire story up with a lie."

"I know, England," Nikki admitted. "He has told so many lies in the past. The truth was hitting me in my face, and I ignored it. I wanted to ignore it because he's so handsome and so fine. I wanted to believe all that he was telling me. Time after time he lied, and I continued to love him.

"I feel so bad," Nikki continued. "I'm trying to forgive myself. I have allowed him to come into my world and turn it upside down. I am an All-American Honor Student who has Ivy League schools fighting over me—promising me a rewarding college life and helping me to fulfill my long-term career goals. I almost threw that away last night. If the police had caught me and taken me to the police station, my life would have been all over. That truly would have been a bitter pill for my folks to swallow."

"Girl, look on the bright side," replied England. "You didn't get caught by the police. If I had a boyfriend from another school, I too would have probably tried to surprise him, especially when he got me believing that I was the only one. You didn't do anything wrong, so stop blaming yourself. Calvin is at fault here. He should have told you he was involved with someone else. I know—guys don't tell you that part. They just try to play the field and hope they don't get caught. People kept telling him not to get involved with China, but he ignored all the warnings. She even gave him warning signs. Like you, he ignored them."

"Calvin has been sleeping with her since day one," England continued. "I guess she was so good he just kept going back for more. At some point he didn't care what people were saying. Calvin and Ken were best friends, and they still may be. However, they do not hang like they used to. Ken appears to be going through some type of change and Calvin does not understand his position right now, so he is not calling Ken as much. They both only dated girls who were giving it up. Now that Ken is going through a change and trying to process his actions, he has not been seen with any girls lately. That's definitely put a strain on his relationship with Calvin. Ken is changing for the better. I believe going to church and attending Bible study has slowed Ken down. I am sure it has to be hard, and he really needs friends right now. I can't imagine what it's like to have so much sex, and then all of a sudden realize that fornicating is not what people claim it to be. Now you have to try to fight the urge to give it up."

There was a brief moment of silence. Then Nikki spoke.

"So, England, are you saying you're still a virgin?"

"Yes, I am still a virgin. I am at the age of innocence, where we all are supposed to be. I used to be embarrassed about it because everyone seemed to be doing it except me. But as I observed my peers and listened to how they got dumped after the fact, I'm very proud to be who

I am right now. I am not jealous that my peers are going through so much pain right now. I am not upset that I still have my virginity and they don't. I'm just glad that God helped to keep me. I have been tempted many times, but my relationship with God has been sustained. Of course, sex will come to be a big part of my life when I'm married. I see pain among my peers who are sexually active. We also have so many HIV cases at my school. You never know who has it because they aren't going to tell you, but they will pass it on to you."

All of this was something for Nikki to think about. As England continued to talk, Nikki drifted in and out of the conversation. Finally, Nikki asked England what she was doing around 6:00.

"Girl, I'm not doing anything but getting with Gabby. We may hang out at her house or something," said England.

"Well, I would like to take you out to dinner for saving me last night and Gabby can come too."

"Cool. I'll call and see if she is game. But even if she isn't go, I'll meet you. So where do you want to meet?"

"You call it. What do you feel like?" asked Nikki. There was a pause. "I tell you what. Don't worry. Let me come up with a plan and I'll call you later, England," exclaimed Nikki.

"Great! I'll talk with you then."

England was happy that Nikki was able to evaluate her situation last night and think about the damage it could have caused her future. After the girls got off the phone, England called Gabby back to see what was going on with Ken.

"Hello!" shouted Gabby.

"What's your problem? Why are you yelling?"

"What took you so long to call me back, chick?"

"Well, I got in a deep conversation with Nikki, and then she invited us to dinner tonight," said England. "She said she wanted to thank me for saving her butt."

"Well, you know God had to be looking down on her because China and her gang were supposed to have eaten her alive!"

"Yes, I know," replied England. "He was looking down on me, too, because Ken and I helped her get out of the situation. Boy, look-uh-here, that was scary. One day somebody is going to crack down on China and her gang with her nasty self."

"Hopefully one day she'll wake up," said Gabby. She is blind and acting the devil's advocate!"

"Don't start preaching, Gabby!" said England. "However, it's scary to be used and know you're being used. What a shame. Okay, why did Ken want to meet us?"

"Well, he said he had to tell us something that was very important," exclaimed Gabby.

"Well, I wonder what that's about. How did he sound?"

"I wasn't aware of how he was sounding because I had several calls coming in at one time. I was bouncing from one call to the next, so I just said okay."

"Alright, I guess we'll meet at our favorite place huh?" replied England.

"Yeah!"

"Okay, pick me up. Better yet, I'll drive."

"Bye."

Chapter 12

Gabby and England

Ken decided not to meet the girls at their favorite spot because of the news he had for them. He knew it was not going to be a pleasant lunch and he was making sure there weren't going to be any loud outbursts. As he contemplated the situation, he thought he should probably have told them about his change of plans in a more private setting. Ken started to get nervous as he backed out of the driveway. Once on the street, he called England.

"Hello!"

"Hey, England, have y'all left the house yet?"

"Yes, we just pulled out of the driveway."

"Well, I have a change of plans."

"What is it?"

"I was wondering if both of you could come over to my house because it will be a much quieter place to talk."

"Okay, I have no problem with that. We're on our way."

As England hung up her phone, she was thinking she'd only been to Ken's house one time. As she was lost in thought, Gabby was calling her name. England finally came out of her daze and acknowledged her.

"What, girl!"

"Land, what's wrong with you?" asked Gabby. "I called your name three times!"

"Sorry, girl, I was in thought."

58

"What were you thinking about?"

"Well, Ken wants us to come to his house instead of going to the spot," said England. So, I was thinking about the last time I was over to his house. His mom was so cool and carefree."

"Why does Ken want to change the meeting place?"

"I don't know," said England, "I can only assume that this info is going to be very juicy."

The girls both became silent while the music played softly in the background. Ken pulled back into the driveway and ran into the house searching for his mother. He found her in the kitchen making a snack for her and his dad.

"Mom!" yelled Ken. "I've invited England and Gabby over for some deep conversation. I was supposed to have met them at our favorite hangout, but I thought it would be best to do this in a more private setting, so I invited them here."

"I'm not hard of hearing. "What do you need me to do?"

"I need you to fix up two or three of your best calming snacks, because this is going to be a rocky ride. And maybe I should light one of your scented candles—one with a relaxing aroma."

"So, you are going to tell them about Calvin?"

"Yes, and I dread this," said Ken. "I've been putting it off, hoping that Calvin would do it."

"I know, son, but it's going to be okay. I'm sorry that Calvin put you in this situation, but you're doing the right thing and your dad, and I are here to support you."

"I know you are, Mom."

Ken left the kitchen so his mom could start preparing the snacks. Ken's mom had always liked England, ever since the first day she met her. She always wanted Ken to date someone like her. But Ken didn't find those types of girls all that interesting. However, she was glad he was still friends with England and Gabby. As she worked on the snacks, she thought of the pain that Ken was experiencing and hoping that he understood why he must change his ways and walk closer with the Lord. Although the Lord allows grief, He will also show compassion. Her thoughts were on the Book of Lamentations, Chapter three. This would be a difficult task for her son, but he must be strong and carry it out.

There was a ring. Ken briskly walked to the door and opened it.

He greeted them both with a hug, inviting the girls in and leading them to the patio overlooking the pool. He asked England about Nikki.

"England, how is Nikki?" he asked.

"Oh, she's okay. But I think she had the scare of her life."

"Yeah, I think I would have been afraid myself in a place where I didn't know anyone, and all of a sudden I'm caught in the middle of a fight."

"That was crazy," said Gabby.

Ken tried to change the subject.

"Well, are you girls ready for some snacks?"

"Yes," said England.

"And may I have some water?" asked Gabby.

"Of course," said Ken.

Ken left the screened patio to go get the snacks.

Gabby said, "England, he looks a little uneasy."

"Yeah, he does! I wonder what's going on."

"I don't know, but I think this is big," said Gabby.

Gabby's left leg started to shake.

"Well, I'd better go to the bathroom," announced England. "You know how I get when I become nervous. And I feel a pee coming on. I'll be back."

England whisked through the door and down the hall to the bathroom. She remembered everything about this house because of her secret love for Ken. While England was in the bathroom, Ken's mom came out with the snacks and Ken was right behind her carrying drinks on a silver tray.

"Well, hello Gabby."

"Hello, Ms. Cole, how are you today?"

"I'm great. What about you?"

"Just fine."

"And your parents?"

"Like two lovebirds."

She laughed.

"Where did England disappear to?" said Ken.

"She went to the bathroom," said Gabby.

"She remembered how to get to the bathroom, huh?" said Ken.

"I guess," said Gabby.

Gabby and Mrs. Cole were enjoying small talk when England arrived at the entrance to the patio. Ken looked up and smiled at England.

"Well, did you find the bathroom?" asked Ken.

"Yes, I believe I did," answered England.

"Hello, Ms. Cole."

"Well, hello to you, England," replied Mrs. Cole. "It's a pleasure to have you in our home again. How have you been?"

"Been great! What about you and Mr. Cole?"

"We're well and we are highly favored by the Lord."

"Truly that's blessing."

"Mom made some special snacks for us. This right here is her perfect warm salmon dip, this right here is her special shrimp-in-a blanket, and these are stuffed mushrooms," bragged Ken.

"Wow, it all looks so yummy," said England.

"All of it is, you just wait until it hits your palate," said Ken.

"Well, thanks Ms. Cole for going through all this trouble of preparing lunch for us," said England.

"Yeah! Thanks! This is just awesome," said Gabby.

"This was not a problem. I love to cook, and I especially love preparing meals for my son's pretty friends."

"Thanks!" the girls said in unison.

"Okay, I am going to leave you guys so you can talk. If you need us, we'll be in the study."

As Ken's mom said her last words, Ken's father entered the patio.

"Hello, my peeps!" Mr. Cole said, trying to be cool.

The girls started laughing at Mr. Cole trying to fit in.

"Hello!" everyone said in unison.

"Who do we have here?" asked Mr. Cole.

"Dad, you met England way back when, and this is her best friend Gabby," said Ken.

"How are you girls doing?"

"We're doing great!"

"Okay, I think I'll go and have lunch with my wife. It was nice seeing you, England, and nice meeting you, Gabby."

"Same here, Mr. Cole."

As the girls prepared their plates, Ken fixed the drinks and prayed in silence, hoping that God would get him through this.

"So, Ken, what's the big secret you have to tell us?"

"It's no secret," replied Ken.

"Okay, just tell us," said England.

"Well, I just don't know how to say something like this, so if it comes out crazy just forgive me, but first let me try some of this good old food."

As they ate, no one said a word. Either the food was very good, or they all were holding their breath. Gabby was wondering what this news could be that had Ken so nervous and afraid. England was also secretly watching Ken's body language. She figured whatever the news was it wasn't good. She knew when something was bothering Ken. She'd studied him for a long time. She could tell when he was hiding something.

After devouring a few pieces of shrimp-in-a-blanket, Ken just blurted out: "Calvin has HIV!"

The room got quiet, and the girls froze where they were. Gabby had her mouth open, ready to take a bite of the salmon dip and crackers, and England missed her mouth with her drink, which splattered all over the front of her blouse. Ken ran to the bathroom for a towel. He came back and started blotting the stains on England's blouse. England snatched the towel.

"What did you say?" exclaimed England.

Ken looked down towards the floor.

"I said Calvin has HIV."

"How long have you known this, Ken?" asked Gabby.

"For about two months. The reason I didn't say anything about it is because I tried to convince Calvin to tell all the girls he'd been involved with, but it was taking him too long. I knew he needed time to absorb this information, as well as try to accept the fact that his life is going to change."

"Does he know you're telling us?" inquired England.

"Yes."

"Wow, I feel like I was run over by a dump truck," remarked Gabby. "This is unbelievable!"

The room became very quiet once again, as thoughts ran through their heads. The only thing England could think about was the fact that Calvin had slept with so many girls. How was he going to prepare himself to tell them? Would he tell them? What about Nikki?

England glanced at Gabby.

Gabby was thinking that she could have been one of those girls who slept with Calvin. Calvin was a very attractive young man with a lot of energy. He always had a lot of girls waiting in line just to spend time with him. Gabby kept saying to herself, "It could have been me!" She thought of the song by the Clark Sisters, "It could have been me; it would have been me if it wasn't for the Lord."

"How long has Calvin known?" asked Gabby.

"That I cannot tell you," said Ken. "I knew he had to get his physical before school started and he did that probably in July or August. But I don't really know. I just knew he was acting strange a couple of weeks after he got his physical. He started telling me that I was getting a little soft because I wasn't chasing girls like I used to. I explained to him that sooner or later one becomes tired of chasing girls and realizes there is much more to life than some tail. I knew who I was, and I also knew that I could get a girl. I just chose to slow my roll and concentrate on other things in life. I also knew that having sex now was wrong. After talking to the pastor about my behavior and activities, he showed me certain Bible scriptures that empowered my thoughts. However, reading the Bible did not make me stop automatically. I had to work on myself and be by myself to understand who I was. I had to read and pray every day for help. Although I had had plenty of girlfriends, I was embarrassed about my behavior and the games I played. For me, it was a game. We played girls as if we did not have a heart. We told them what they wanted to hear just to have sex with them. We used to sit back and laugh about this and talk about how easy it was to get sex. We preyed on the weak girls—girls whose parents were going through a divorce, girls who were being raised by one parent, girls whose parents did not give them the attention they needed, and girls who just had low self-esteem. I wanted to help Calvin, but he was so far gone. I tried to get him to go to church and talk with our pastor, but he wouldn't listen. I tried to show him proof that what we were doing was against God's will and plan for us. He told me that I was jealous because he was getting more than I was. After that, our relationship became strained."

"How did he manage to tell you?" asked England.

"Calvin missed a couple of days from school, and I went by his house to check on him," Ken continued. "His mom answered the door with tears in her eyes. I asked her what was wrong, and she told me she was not at liberty to say and that I needed to talk with Calvin. She directed me to his room, where he was lying across the bed. I looked around the room and saw all of these bottles of pills. I went a little closer to see if I could read the labels, but I didn't know how to pronounce the name of the medicines. However, I did remember the spelling. I told Calvin that I dropped by to check on him because he had missed two days of school. I asked him what was going on and he told me that he had a cold, and I was not to get too close because I might catch it, so I backed up. I told him that I picked up his homework and gave him the chapters we'd covered in class. He told me to leave it on the dresser because he needed to get some rest, so I left."

"So, he didn't tell you!" Gabby said.

"No, I actually found out on my own," Ken went on. "I called the drug store a week later and told them about this drug that I was doing research on, and they gave me the information I needed. The pharmacist told me the drug was for patients who were diagnosed with HIV. I thought he'd made a mistake, so I called another pharmacy and they told me the same thing. I was speechless and confused. I pulled over to the side of the road to collect myself. I didn't know what to do. I went home, ran to my room, and prayed for this not to be true. I didn't sleep for two days straight. I wondered when Calvin was planning on telling me and what I would say. I thought he would have come to me for support, but he didn't. I wondered how he contracted the disease, especially since he always wore a condom. All kinds of stuff was running through my mind. He and I were just the same—we loved and enjoyed sex. How could this have happened to him and not me? I had so many questions."

"When did you finally confront him?"

"After I saw him with Nikki."

"What!"

"Yes!" Ken exclaimed. "I went to his house the next day to talk, hoping he would tell me instead of me telling him. I went to his room, and he was asleep. I looked at another bottle of his meds and decided to call the pharmacy and ask about that drug. I went out of his room near the staircase and made the phone call. Again, the pharmacist told me the proper name for the drug and its purpose. Now I was sure that Calvin was infected with HIV. I went back to his room and watched him sleep. I stayed until he woke up."

"Then?"

"Well, I asked him why he'd been acting so strangely, as if he was addicted to something. He asked me how I liked Nikki and if I thought she was hot. I told him to talk to me. I reminded him that we were best friends and always would be, no matter what. He just looked at me. He said that I was a trip and shook his head.

Then I said, 'Okay, Calvin, what's going on?' He didn't answer. I stood up and walked toward the dresser. I picked up a bottle of his meds and said, 'What's this medicine for?' He jumped up and snatched the bottle out of my hand telling me it was none of my business. I could tell he hadn't taken any of the medicine, because the bottle appeared to have the same amount in it as when I saw it the first time."

"What happened next?"

"It got quiet," said Ken. "We sat and sat and sat. Then he told me with tears streaming down his face. I cried along with him, trying to comfort him and let him know that he could beat this thing. He told me that he found out when he got his physical last summer, but it didn't hit him until he got sick one day at school. He knew he had to make some changes in his life. He said he had to find out who gave him this awful disease. I told him that he had to tell his partners, so they could get checked. He said he couldn't tell anyone that he was HIV positive. I knew he was hurting and embarrassed, but it was their right to know. The same way he wanted to know who gave it to him. I am sure those girls he was with would want to know that he was infected."

Gabby stated, "I'm so blessed. Here I am, tripping over the fact that I was still a virgin in the 12th grade. Now I am even more proud of my virginity. I could have been in the same situation as Nikki and the rest of Calvin's girlfriends. I'm totally afraid for all of them. I pray that they all didn't sleep with Calvin, and, if they did, perhaps they used a condom, although that is not 100% safe either."

"I read that most teenagers are sexually active before they leave high school and half of them leave with some type of transmitted disease," England remarked. "And it doesn't get better on the college campuses. We have to continue to be protective of ourselves when we go off to college. This is wild and crazy."

"More than anything, we have to put our trust in God and realize that God has a plan for all of us," said Gabby.

Ken agreed. "This is ugly! I just want Calvin to talk to the girls he slept with. He needs to give them an opportunity to save their lives. He does not need to wait any longer! The earlier they know, the better off they'll be."

"Ken, you and Calvin have been with so many girls. Are you getting tested as well?" asked England.

"Yes, I have been with a lot of girls, and I've been tested several times. I was getting tested before I found out about Calvin. When my doctor asked me about how many sex partners I've had, I had to be honest with him. He told me then that I needed to slow my roll. He told me life was not about sex. Rather, it is about serving God and being in training to be a great provider for my family. At that time, I thought this was lame. I didn't want to hear that. I thought I was on top of the world."

"He wasn't supposed to say that as your physician."

"He can say that because he's my dad's best friend. So, he's just like my uncle."

"So, what really slowed you down?" asked Gabby.

This was a big question that Gabby asked. But Ken knew he could not answer it truthfully, because he still wanted England to be his friend. If he spoke honestly, he knew he would not have a chance with England in the future.

"Well, after talking to our pastor, I decided to slow things down a bit. No, I should say I stopped altogether. I knew what I was doing was wrong and not acceptable to God."

England looked Ken in the eye. Underneath her breath she called him a liar. She rolled her eyes but did not say a word. Then she grinned bitterly. Ken thought he had fooled her, but he didn't. Quietness filled the room.

"How is Calvin's mom taking this news?"

"She's devastated!" said Ken. "She has had to raise him by herself. Sometimes she would work long hours and he'd be home a lot by himself. I guess that would be somewhat boring."

"And hunting down girls occupied his time?" asked Gabby.

"No, I wouldn't say it like that, Gabby!"

"Well, how would you say it? That it was just something to do?"

"Calm down, Gabby, I was just saying that he had time to do what he wanted to do. We both did," said Ken.

Quietness filled the room once again.

Gabby was thinking back to the time she was dating Calvin. She thought he was so cool, smart, and good looking. She thought about the girls who might have contracted the disease from him. She thought about how many people were going to be hurt because of those actions. AIDS is the sixth leading cause of teenage deaths. She could not blame Calvin alone. She knew she had to also lay some blame on his partners. She also thought about how he would look at her now. Could he face her, knowing that she knew? She took one more look at herself and realized how she had stood tall against alcohol, drugs, and sex, just by being true to herself. This had not been an easy road to travel. Gabby thought about all the dates the girls would talk about during lunchtime, and how she had to listen to each story that was being told. Gabby wanted to be a part of the action just like any other teenage girl.

Gabby was startled as England's cell phone rang. England answered it.

"Hello this is England."

"Hi, England, this is Nikki."

"Hi Nikki. I'm glad you called."

Ken and Gabby looked at England.

"We're going to have to meet another time," England continued, "because I'm in a meeting and I'm afraid that I may not be finished before six."

Nikki reassured England that it was okay because she had something she had to do this evening as well. England was relieved.

"Okay guys, what am I supposed to tell Nikki?" asked England. "She just cancelled our dinner for this evening. Well, we both cancelled, but at some point, I will have to see her again. Do I tell her, or wait to see if Calvin is going to tell her?"

"Calvin is not going to tell her," said Ken.

"Well, what do I do?"

"This is hard," replied Gabby.

"How long do you think you can hold out on her?" asked Ken.

"I don't know," said England. "I just know that I don't need to talk with her until we hear what Calvin is going to do."

"He just said that Calvin is not going to tell her!" exclaimed Gabby.

"So, we need to tell her!" said England.

"Yep, I understand what you're saying, England. You have a big mouth, and you take other people's problems to heart," said Ken.

"What does that mean?"

"It means you talk too much."

"Okay, let's give it some thought because obviously this is too much for us to handle," said Gabby.

"I agree," said England. "Let's go home, Gabby!"

"Ken, thanks for telling us, although you should have told us sooner," said Gabby.

"Don't make him think he has done us any favors, because he should have told us sooner."

"England, don't be so hard. You must be compassionate right now. This is his best friend, and they're like brothers!" exclaimed Gabby.

"If you say so. Bye, Ken."

England walked away.

Gabby apologized for England's rudeness as Ken walked her to the door. England was already in the car when Gabby got in.

"England, what is your freaking problem?"

"Girl, don't be tripping; you know Ken is just a bigger whore than Calvin."

"So, we know this, but that does not give you a reason to be rude to the boy."

"I wasn't rude! He should have told us this a long time ago. It did not just happen! He was supposed to be our friend, too, and he could have stopped a lot of girls from sleeping with Calvin. Do you know how many lives are at risk? Have you thought about that, Miss Prissy?"

Gabby did not say a word. England drove in complete silence. All she could think about was how she was going to look Calvin in his face knowing this kind of information. She could not begin to even think about how she was going to deliver this type of news to her parents.

This was one reason why Gabby had abstained from sex. People were dying all over the place from this virus and the girls at school had not heard that wake-up call yet. You would think people would want to hold off until marriage. NO, no, no! They want it now and as much as they can get.

While Gabby was in her thoughts, England was thinking about how many seniors were active. She thought about an article that she read last month in the newspaper pertaining to sex and teenagers. The author stated that more than 60% of seniors have indulged in sex at least once before graduation, and this was on a national level. Wow!

When Gabby got home, she went upstairs and lay across her bed. She was torn emotionally and started to cry softly. She could not believe this was happening. She would read articles and listen to the news about HIV/AIDS, but never ever thought someone close to her would have it. She didn't know how to address her own concerns. She was discombobulated and just wanted to rest and gather her thoughts.

She wanted to fall off to sleep but had too much on her mind. She knew she had to talk with Calvin one-on-one. She had to hurry up and calm down so she could think rationally. She knew she had to approach Calvin from a different angle, but "how" was the question. She wondered if she should tell her parents. She knew they would be supportive and speak from their hearts. She knew they would not intentionally misinform her. Then again, this would be a difficult topic for any parent. Gabby was not ready just yet to tell them. However, if England told her parents Gabby knew that England's mom would be on that phone trying to make contact with her mom.

Gabby jumped out of bed and called England.

"Hey England, did you tell your mom yet?"
"No!"
"Why are you snapping at me!"
"I am just tense right now. I know if I tell my mom she's going to freak out. Did you?"
"No, I was trying to find a way to give them such news. With Calvin being sick and not taking his meds, I get the feeling he's going to go downhill fast. I was also trying to find words to say to Calvin. He has not told any of those females and I think they need to know. I just don't know how to go about this. First, I thought I needed to talk to Calvin one on one. Then I thought maybe Ken would get him to tell these girls to go get checked, or get a blood test, or something. I'm

just torn right now."

"Well, Gabby, don't try to do this by yourself," said England. "Just go to God in prayer and He will direct your thoughts. The idea will start burning and it will want to be born. Although Calvin is going to be embarrassed, he is going to be happy that you came to him. I think he would want that."

"This is so hard, even though he dumped me."

"Let's look at the bright side, Gabby. Aren't you glad God stepped in right in the nick of time? Aren't you glad that you had the self-control that was given to you by God? Aren't you glad that you're a Christian and was able to lean on those scriptures in time of need? Aren't you glad you thought before you proceeded? Aren't you glad you are not in Nikki's, China's, and those other girls' shoes? Girl, God has you covered."

"Wow, that was a mouthful. I'm grateful, England, but I feel their pain even now and they don't know that their life is getting ready to change."

"Hey, I'm sorry for saying all of those mean things," England replied. "I allowed my emotions to get the best of me and I wasn't thinking. But I still believe that Ken should have told us sooner."

"England, I wholeheartedly agree with you. But I do understand Ken's position in all of this when I look at the human side of things."

"What human side?" exclaimed England. "There is no human side! I know they're best friends, and he's going to stick with Calvin until the end. But Calvin owes the people the right to know what's up, even if he doesn't want people to know. I know this is painful, but I can't say I feel his pain because I am not in his shoes or Ken's. I just know that Calvin owes society the truth. Once they know, all will know, and he will not be spreading the disease any longer, at least not in this town."

Silence once again. Then England spoke up.

"Girl, I am just getting worked up again about this. Do you know approximately how many girls we're talking about? This is going to be a mess once everyone gets a hold of this! This boy is academically intelligent, but what happened to his common sense?"

"He had a beast in him that wanted to escape," exclaimed Gabby.

"Beast! Girl! I got a beast in me that can't escape! Now that this has hit home, I'm glad that I practice abstinence, although I felt forlorn at times."

"Well, you've been on dates."

"Yes, and most of them were ready to go all the way."

"I think that's what they think they're supposed to do," Gabby said, "with their clueless selves."

"I feel as if we have had this conversation before," said England.

"Yeah, we said that boys think dating is about sex. Having sex makes them look good in front of others."

"They like to feel the acceptance of their peers, or should I say comrades."

"I'm glad that Ken finally opened his eyes to see that there is more to life than sex," replied England. "Sex is a part of the human life, yet we must be true to ourselves when we decide if we're ready to experience such a thing."

"Have you ever been in the situation of wanting to do it but were afraid?" asked Gabby.

England was lost in thought.

"You remember Tony, the football player in ninth grade?"

"Mumm!"

"Well, I wanted to make passionate love to that boy," England remarked. "He was so fine, and his body looked like it belonged on the cover of GQ magazine. He had all the girls checking him out. Everyone thought he was the bomb. When he looked at me with those green eyes, girl, I thought I was going to heaven! He walked so smooth with his chest out, like he was in somebody's army. I was saying, 'Yes sir! Major, Corporal, Lieutenant Tony McKlester!' Boy, was I on a roll dreaming of making love with him. I often wondered what it would be like to just give myself to him. Would he remember me when we grew older and wiser? Would he tease me because I allowed him to enter me? Would he love me? Would he tell his friends? And when they saw me, would they laugh and call me names just like they were doing the other girls?"

The girls were silent for a moment.

"England, that was a wild trip you just took. But I feel like we have allowed ourselves to feel bad because we are not having sex. You and I know the consequences we would have to pay if we decided to go down that road. Sometimes I feel lonely not being able to spend time with the boyfriend that I don't have. And sometimes I'm glad that I don't have one, because he would cause a lot of confusion in my life. I don't want to have to confront or fight anyone over a boy. I wish I could just have someone to talk to, someone I'm interested in."

"What about Matthew?"

"Girl, Matt is a friend," Gabby said. "He is a good friend who's working very hard at fulfilling his dream."

"How come we can't run into more boys like Matt?" asked England. "Why do they all have to be so selfish and so sexual?"

"I think it has to do with a lot of this music, and these music videos."

"Let's not forget the partial nudity we see on commercials."

"Yeah, in a way they're saying it's okay to be nude in front of other people," said Gabby, "or it's okay to have open sex in front of a crowd."

"The devil has his hands on the entertainment industry like never before."

"Everything that is being created today is so profane, so sexual. If you listen to it long enough, it will get you in the mood to do something you will regret later."

"Thank you, God, for the guidance. Without you we would be disoriented. With you, we are on course. The course you want us to travel."

England's phone had another call coming in.

"Hold on, Gabby, I've got another call," said England. "Hello."

"Hey girl, this is Nikki. What are you doing?"

"I'm talking with Gabby. What's up with you?"

"Nothing. I just wanted to see if you want to come over."

"Yes, but can I bring Gabby?"

"Of course!"

"Okay, we should be there around seven."

"Well, you will be on time."

"On time for what?"

"Dinner."

"Okay, see you then."

"Bye."

England clicked back over to Gabby.

"Gabby."

"What!"

"Nikki wants us to come over about seven."

"Us! What do you mean us?"

"Well, you know I'm not going over there by myself to deliver this type of news."

"Why did you tell her we were coming tonight?"

"Well, I'm ready to get this over with." said England. "You know Calvin is not going to tell her. And I will not sleep until she is told."

"I need to talk with Calvin first."

"Okay, just stop by his house on your way over here."

"I want to give him a chance to tell her," said Gabby.

"He has had all of these months to tell her, and he hasn't," said England. "Why do you think he's going to tell her now?"

"Hopefully, I can get through to him, and he will want to tell her and the others."

"Well, good luck, Gabby. But I think you're wasting your time."

Gabby rolled her eyes.

"Okay, I'll talk with you later."

"Bye, Gabby, and be safe."

Gabby hung up the phone.

After getting off the phone with England, Gabby decided she would pray before going to Calvin's house. Gabby's mom entered the room while she was praying. She stood at the door silently. Gabby got up and stared into her mom's eyes. Gabby's mom put her arms around her as Gabby sobbed. Gabby's mom assured her that everything was going to be all right.

"Mom, I need to go to Calvin's house, then to England's house, and my final destination will be Nikki's house."

"Well, I know that something is wrong. Please tell me Gabby, because you do not have to go through this alone, whatever it is. More than anything, you don't need to be driving when you're upset. You must stay focused when you're driving."

"Mom, don't worry. I'm fine, but a friend is in trouble, and he needs my help. Once I get this straightened out with God's help, I will tell you. But all parties involved need to know first."

"Okay, I don't speak your language, but I will be here if you need me."

"Thanks, Mom."

"Be careful and drive safely. Call me throughout your visits."

"I won't be long, but I will call you."

"I love you, Gabby."

"You too."

Gabby went downstairs, grabbed her keys and purse, and headed out the door. Gabby was frightened, but she stayed focused and talked to God all the way to Calvin's house. She asked God for support and to give her the words to say to Calvin. She wanted Calvin to be open to her suggestions, so it would be easier for her to tell her folks.

Gabby got out of the car and rang the doorbell.

"Who is it?"

"It's Gabby, Ms. Mitchell."

"Hold on, Gabby."

Ms. Mitchell unlocked the door and invited Gabby in.

"Hi, Ms. Mitchell."

"Hello. How are you?"

"I am doing okay, how about you?"

"Well, my life could be better, but I have to play the cards that were dealt."

I'm sure it will get better," Gabby said. "Just have faith."

"Okay, faith."

"How is Calvin? I came by to see him."

"Calvin is being Calvin. Let me call upstairs and see if you can go up."

Calvin's phone rang. And rang. And rang.

"Hmmm. Calvin is not picking up the phone," said Ms. Mitchell.

"Maybe he's in the bathroom."

"Maybe."

Calvin's mom went upstairs and found him on the bathroom floor. She yelled downstairs and told Gabby to call 911. Gabby did what she asked, then ran upstairs. When Gabby got to the bathroom, Calvin's mom was doing CPR. Gabby got some cool towels and placed them on Calvin's head. His body was burning up. It felt like it was on fire. The paramedics rang the doorbell and Gabby ran downstairs to let them in. She pointed in the direction of the stairs. They ran up the stairs with their equipment. Gabby was right behind them. They took over as Ms. Mitchell stepped out the way.

They asked her a lot of questions, and Ms. Mitchell told them that

Calvin was HIV positive. When Gabby heard that coming from his mother; it really hit her like a ton of bricks. She knew he had HIV, but to hear his mother say it really hit home. She was sure she was having a dream this time.

"Okay ma'am, we have him stable right now. We're going to take him to the hospital," said one of the paramedics.

"Ms. Mitchell, I will drive you to the hospital," said Gabby.

"Okay Gabby, thanks."

They both grabbed their keys and purses and ran to the car. Gabby put on her emergency lights to let drivers know she was in a hurry. She had learned this from her mom. When they got to the hospital, Gabby called England first. England would call Ken and Nikki, while Gabby called her mom.

"Mom, mom," yelled Gabby.

"Hi, Gabby, what's wrong?"

"I'm at the hospital with Calvin and his mom."

"What happened?"

"Calvin's mom went upstairs to see if it was okay for me to go up, and she found him passed out on the floor. I called the paramedics."

"Is he going to be all right? Do I need to come to the hospital?"

"Yes, we are at Roosevelt Medical Center."

"Okay, sweetie, I'm on my way."

Gabby hung up the phone and went to sit with Ms. Mitchell. Ms. Mitchell was crying.

"Did you know that Calvin was HIV positive?" she asked Gabby.

"Yes, ma'am."

"He didn't tell many people, although I told him he must tell those girls who he had dated and was dating."

"I'm sure he was going to tell them," said Gabby. "He just had to first accept it himself."

"Yes, I guess."

"Ms. Mitchell, was Calvin taking his medicine?"

"No, not like he should have."

"Well, maybe this is going to be just a small setback for him, one he can overcome."

"Gabby, I hope so. But I need your prayers."

"I've always prayed, and I will continue to do so, Ms. Mitchell."

Ken and England came through the double doors asking questions.

Ken put his arm around Ms. Mitchell to help calm her down. Thirty minutes later, Gabby's parents and Nikki came through the doors. Gabby looked at Nikki and then at England with her mouth opened. However, England did not see Nikki, nor was she paying attention to Gabby. Gabby realized this was going to be a long night.

Chapter 13

Gabby and England

When England turned around to face Gabby, Nikki was staring her in her face.

"Wow! How did you get here?"

"I drove."

"By yourself!"

"Yes!"

Calvin's mom was already in conversation with Gabby's parents. As England questioned Nikki, Nikki was trying to hear what Calvin's mom was telling the McWright's. Between the sobbing and the tears, she couldn't really hear. Nikki's heart started beating fast and she felt faint. England was trying to think on her feet. Before she and Ken rushed off to the hospital, England called Nikki to cancel their dinner date once again. This time England talked a little too much because of her fear and concern for Gabby, but not too much for Calvin.

"England, what's going on?" demand Nikki. "Why is his mother so upset? Why did he have to come to the hospital? Was he in an accident? What's going on?"

"Well, Nikki I was supposed to tell you this before tonight," replied England, "but I just could not...I don't know...I just didn't know how to say it and I wanted to also respect your privacy, but...I thought you should know."

"Know what?"

"Well, do you want to go for a walk?" said England.

Nikki started yelling and demanding that England tell her right then and there.

"Nikki, I really think we need to talk about this somewhere else!"

Nikki continued to yell, this time a little louder. Ken started walking towards them and Calvin's mom rushed over and said, "My son has HIV!"

Nikki didn't get it all because of the crying and the moaning that was coming from the mouth of Calvin's mom.

"Excuse me, I didn't hear you, ma'am."

"I said Calvin has HIV!"

Nikki could not move. She was as still as a mannequin in a window. England put her arms around Nikki to console her, but Nikki acted like a crazy person. She started screaming and ran out the hospital door.

England called her name, with Ken right behind her. They finally caught Nikki and grabbed a hold of her. Nikki was fighting and crying at the same time. England kept apologizing to Nikki. Ken held Nikki very close and whispered softly in her ear. Nikki was out of breath. Feeling sorry for Nikki, England's tears started rolling down her cheeks. Seeing this kind of pain was very disturbing to both Ken and England.

"Why did this have to happen?" asked Nikki, in tears.

"I don't know," said Ken.

"I can't believe this isn't some kind of soap opera!"

"Nikki, I know you have slept with Calvin, so I think it would be wise if you got tested to make sure you're not infected," said Ken.

"I've been so stupid, so foolish to sleep with him!"

"Don't say that!" said Ken. "You are not any of those things."

"We all make mistakes, Nikki," said England.

Nikki looked at England in a very vicious way.

"We! How in the hell can you say we, when you've never made a mistake," replied Nikki? "You are still pure and not haunted by demons."

"Nikki don't be so mean," said England calmly. "I have tried to warn you since the day I met you, but I guess I was too late."

"Yeah, I guess you were."

"Nikki, England has only tried to be a friend," said Ken. "She just could not come right out and tell you anything. She wanted to talk to you many times, but I thought it was only fair that Calvin tell you himself."

"I cannot believe this. It can't be real. This has to be a dream."

"No, it's not a dream, so wake up!"

"Why didn't Calvin tell me this?"

The three of them sat on the curb, heads pressed against each other's shoulders.

"I am sure he wanted to tell you," Ken said, "but there probably were several factors involved. First, he was in denial. Second, he was embarrassed. Third, he knew that the information would get out and he was not ready to handle all the questions and harsh accusations."

"Nikki, I know you feel like you've been hit with a ton of bricks," added England, "but you really need to know your status. So, don't wait, because time is moving on and we don't know how long Calvin has been HIV positive."

"I don't even know where to start. My parents can't find out, and what about my friends? If they find out that I even slept with Calvin, I will be ridiculed. I would probably get kicked out of the academy. What about China? Does she know?"

"Nikki, you have so many questions that neither England nor I can answer. Those are questions you have to ask Calvin, and we don't know how sick Calvin is."

"What do you know?" asked Nikki.

"I know Calvin is sick and he has caused a great deal of pain to all parties involved, which includes his family, his friends, his girlfriends and their families."

"So, he has had a lot of sexual partners?"

"I am not at liberty to say."

England looked at Ken and just shook her head. Ken looked at England hoping she would help him out, but she didn't. She understood Ken knew much more than he was willing to say.

After an hour of sitting on the curb, they decided to walk back to the hospital. As they walked, they were lost in their own thoughts.

Ken realized that could have been him lying in the gurney, because he was just as dangerous as Calvin. They lived in the same bubble. They completed each other's thoughts and sentences. They did their dirt together most of the time. They slept with a lot of girls. They were known as the bad boys in the school. They enjoyed their title and lived up to the name.

England was thinking back on when she and Gabby first met the bad boys. They'd already heard that these boys dated girls and dropped them like flies after they'd scored. Their resumes were all over the school. However, girls still flocked to them as if they were gods.

Nikki thought that she couldn't have HIV because she'd already made plans to go to college and take over her dad's practice. She thought back to the day she met Calvin. He was so fine in his French shirt and jeans, with a diamond stud in one ear. He had white pearly teeth, with the biggest grin you would ever want to see. He didn't look sick at all. He looked as healthy as anyone else.

As they entered the double doors of the hospital, Nikki's heart raced. The sterile smell, the sight of patients in various states of health, and the sound of beeping machines overwhelmed her. She stopped dead in her tracks, her mind tracking with fear and uncertainty.

"Nikki, what's wrong?" asked England.

"I think I'll go home now. I just can't wait here in this hospital."

"You know, I think that is best too," agreed England. "Do you want me to ride with you? I'm sure Ken or Gabby wouldn't mind following us so they can give me a lift."

"No, I'll be just fine. Besides, I need time to think and soak all this in."

"Okay, well call me when you get home safely."

"I will," said Nikki.

"Bye, Nikki, and be safe," said Ken.

England and Ken both walked down to the waiting room to find only Gabby waiting for them. Ken looked down the hall for a nurse or someone else, but they saw no one. They walked down the hall to the nursing station and asked about Calvin. The nurse told them that Calvin was resting, and they should go home and get some rest. They decided to do so since it was past visiting hours.

England rode home with Gabby. They both told Ken goodnight and that they'd see him tomorrow in church.

"Gabby, this has been a night for me," said England. "I'm overwhelmed with all of this. I really don't have words to describe my feelings."

"Whaaat...you out of words? Well, I can understand. I was getting close to Calvin when he dumped me. I thought he was a lunatic and would come running back to me. Then I thought something was wrong with me, not wanting to be with him in that way.

"Being a teenager is too much pressure," replied England. "If I didn't have you as a friend and we didn't share the same beliefs and morals, I don't know if I could have been strong enough to live the life that I'm living. I often thought of having sex. I often thought of being lonely. I often thought of what to say and how to say no when I got stuck in a sticky situation. I used to get weak when a boy kissed me on my neck or blew in my ear. Yep! All of that felt good, but not so good that I would allow someone to put me in a risky situation."

"England, I share your thoughts," said Gabby. "It appears when I'm close to messing up, God just knows when to step in and put a stop to the act before it gets to the next level. I give all the credit to God for covering me when I'm out on dates. It hasn't been all that easy to keep my pants up and my legs closed. I know a lot of girls are having sex, but there are also a lot not having sex. I feel that we are in the popularity group because of what we have decided not to give up."

"As I read the article on the epidemic of STDs," replied England, "I thought about our little group and how blessed we are not to be among those girls who are sexually active."

"What article? What is it talking about?"

"Well, it was an article in the newspaper about two weeks ago. Actually, it has been in the news for the last three weeks straight. Girl, where have you been? Haven't you been watching the news?"

"No, not really! Just tell me what the article mentioned!" said Gabby.

"Okay! The article reported that Georgia was number three for most syphilis cases. In one area of Atlanta, they had a billboard that asked people if they knew their status."

"I tell ya, life is becoming scarier every day. Syphilis is one of those old diseases. I guess it's back on the rise, just like herpes. Are there any symptoms?"

"The article stated that there are four stages," said England. "During the first two you will have some symptoms, such as a painless sore on any body part, but it will go away. However, you still will have the disease—it's just developing into another stage."

"So, people may just dismiss the sore as something else, because it's not painful and it goes away in a number of days?" asked Gabby.

"Yes, probably because people are not going to just run straight to the doctor," replied England. "They are going to work on it themselves. Then it goes away, and they think it is gone bye-bye."

"But it is really moving to the next stage and getting more difficult to treat," said Gabby.

"Mumm, but the sores can come and go for at least a year."

"But in the third stage?" asked Gabby.

"Symptoms may never appear again, but the bacteria are still there. Just lingering on and sucking on the body organs or parts."

"Yuk, that's nasty!" cried Gabby.

"You know, Gabby, my parents have always been openly ready to communicate about sex and diseases. However, we never talked about syphilis. I never asked and they never mentioned it. But we've talked about herpes, HIV, and chlamydia."

"When you asked questions about sex or sexual disease, did you see a certain look on their faces, as if you were doing something you had no business doing, or did they look like they had big question marks on their foreheads?"

"Yeah, I think they probably thought at first that I was engaged in sexual activities," said England, "or they thought I may have a disease."

"My parents always looked crazy, like I was getting ready to tell them something was wrong with me. And that's one reason why I don't ask too many questions. I think too many questions make them nervous and then they start wondering if I'm having sex."

"I know when I leave the room, they start whispering to each other: 'I wonder if my baby is having sex. Please God, don't let her have sex now.' Then they try to calm each other down," said England.

"Parents are a trip," agreed Gabby. "After you ask a question, they don't want to let you out the room. They go on and on. They want you to tell them something incriminating about yourself. So, I reassure them by saying, 'Mom, don't worry, I'm not having sex.' Then one of them may come back and say, 'Well, why are you asking me that question?' It's just too crazy, so I do my own research and answer my own questions because I know they trip when I leave the room."

"Parents have a hard job."

"Not as hard as ours, England."

"Only you would think that, Gabby."

"Why do you say that?"

"Your schedule is so tight you hardly have time for a social life.

"Well, maybe you need to beef yours up," said Gabby.

"No, I like it the way it is."

"I guarantee you if you beef it up," Gabby said, "you won't have time to fantasize about Ken. Furthermore, he may have HIV or AIDS. Who knows!"

"Oh, hell! That was below the belt! You didn't have to go there! You're wrong!"

"You need to stop playing yourself," replied Gabby. "You know you like him; I know you like him, and he does too. So, admit it!"

"I…I…"

"Don't lie, England! Tell the truth and shame the devil!"

"You know what?" England shot back. "You are a witch and I'm ending the conversation!"

"Whateva!"

England knew that Gabby might be telling the truth. Who knew Ken's status? They did know that he had multiple partners and was at high risk of contracting the disease. Recently they had seen his bad behavior change somewhat. But had it really changed, or was Ken simply being careful and more discrete? You can only know a person by what he told you unless you see it for yourself. Should England's feelings change, now that she knew Calvin has HIV and it was a possibility that Ken may be diagnosed with it later?

As the girls rode in silence, they both thought about what was coming next and whether Calvin would pull out of it.

Chapter 14

Gabby

A week had passed and no one mentioned Calvin's condition. Gabby was glad that China was not talking to her or England. China was still mad and wasn't talking to Ken either. Gabby looked at her as she walked through the door of the classroom. To Gabby she looked normal. Gabby stared at China as she went to her seat. The teacher got their attention by preparing to call roll. The teacher went through the roster as usual, but when he got to Calvin's name he stopped and asked out loud, "Has anyone seen Calvin?" No one answered. Then he said, "Guess not." The teacher kept on going down the roll, calling names.

In the meantime, Gabby was thinking about Calvin. She wondered if it would be okay to visit him. She thought of his smile and white teeth and that one dimple on his left cheek. She smiled slightly.

"Girl, what are you smiling about?"

Gabby didn't answer. She'd been in her own world throughout the entire class.

England shoved Gabby's knee with hers and said, "Girl, what are you grinning about?"

Gabby jumped and said, "What is it?"

"Girl, I was asking why you were smiling so hard. You were in a zone."

"Oh, I was just lost in thought."

"Well, you need to pay attention," England persisted. "Mr. Morrow said that you will do your presentation next Thursday and I will go after you."

"Okay, that's cool. I'll be ready."

The bell rang and it was time to go to lunch. Gabby and England went down the street to Burger King and came back with their lunches. During lunch, a group of girls who normally did not sit with Gabby and England came to sit with them. England looked at Gabby, wondering why China's friends were at her table. She knew something was up because these girls didn't like them. They didn't even speak to them. Now they were at the same table trying to eat lunch with them. England was not in the mood for a ruckus. Gabby could not believe their boldness. Gabby also realized this was not the norm and something was getting ready to go down. But what? Ken was headed that way but when he looked up and saw them in plain view, he made a U-turn and took a seat in the corner, making sure he was in full view of them. He wanted to think. As people came through the lunch line, everyone saw this picture. Ken observed the students and the girls. He didn't like what he was thinking, so he decided he would go and join them. He thought this was probably going to be a day that he didn't eat his lunch at this time and in this place.

"What up, England, Gabby!"

"The sky," said England.

"The sun," said Gabby.

"Oh, y'all got jokes," said Monique.

"No, but you definitely got some," said England.

"Nah, we just decided we are going to eat with y'all today."

"Why would you want to do that?" said Gabby.

"Well, we just want to say we are sorry for not taking y'all under our wings and teaching you how to fly," replied Monique.

"We are flying just like a Delta 757 with all 'A's.' You can't fly no better than that," said England. She looked at Gabby. "What do you think, Gabby? You think we missed something?"

"Not a thing, England."

"So, you see, Monique," England continued, "we are stronger flyers who never did and will never need your help. And since you are the pilot of your plane, how about getting up and flying to a new seat, because you are not welcome!"

"England, you always had a big mouth," countered Monique. "You don't realize when people are trying to be nice."

"You and your friends have hated us since middle school," replied England. "Why do you want to be our friends now? It's over with—it's time for us to graduate and move on to bigger and better things."

"Damn, we didn't hate y'all," said Erica, "we just didn't like y'all attitudes, that's all."

"I would ask you why, but it's no concern of mine," replied England. "I just want to eat my lunch in peace, so move! Now!"

England stood up and looked them square in their faces.

"England, we can eat where we want to. You're not the boss of us!"

"Monique, Erica, y'all need to leave," said Ken, chuckling.

"Right now."

Ken rose from his seat, staring Monique in the face. The students in the lunchroom got quiet. Monique rose from her seat. She looked Ken right in his eyes with a grin on her face and said, "I'm not going to let you get me excited, because if I punch you, blood will start squirting everywhere, and I don't want your blood on me."

"Yeah, uh huh, we heard," said Erica.

As the girls got up from the table, they started giggling and mumbling to themselves. The students in the cafeteria started talking again and moving around. Ken was very upset with what Monique said, but he knew he couldn't do anything about it. It was in Ken's best interests not to react to her statement because he would have jeopardized his graduation and scholarship.

Ken sat down. He really wanted to walk out of the cafeteria, but he did not want people to think that Monique had something on him. So, he stayed and picked at his food while Gabby and England ate their meals. After lunch, Gabby checked out to go to a dental appointment. After her appointment she went to the hospital. At the entrance Gabby said hello to the nurses and kept walking. She forgot to sign in and get a visitor's badge. One of the nurses was trying to get Gabby's attention, but Gabby didn't hear her. The nurse followed her to Calvin's room. Gabby didn't see his name on the door. As she was turning around, the nurse was right in her tracks and startled Gabby.

"Young lady, I was trying to get your attention."

"I'm sorry ma'am, I didn't hear you. Do you know where

Calvin's new room is located?"

"Calvin was discharged earlier today."

"Discharged? Does that mean he is better?"

"I don't know, I just know that he is no longer here with us."

"Did he go home?"

"I don't know. Perhaps you should call his mom."

"Okay, ma'am, sorry to ask you so many questions."

"Not a problem."

Gabby and the nurse headed back to the front entrance. Gabby was wondering if Ken knew that Calvin had checked out. She looked at her watch to see what time it was. School was still in session and Ken had about thirty more minutes in his last class. Gabby couldn't wait, so she texted Ken. The text read: *Are you aware that Calvin was discharged from the hospital?* Sending the text put Gabby at ease. However, she knew that Ken was going to have to text her when the teacher was not looking. So she waited for his text while she proceeded to drive home.

Forty minutes passed and no text from Ken. Gabby then speed dialed his number. Ken answered.

"Hello."

"Hey, why didn't you text me back?" Gabby asked.

"Text you back? I didn't get a text from you."

"Well, I texted you about forty minutes ago."

"Okay, I'll check it later," Ken said. "Maybe something happened, and I didn't receive it. What's up?"

"Well, after I left my dental appointment, I went by the hospital to see Calvin, but he was discharged earlier today. Did you know that?"

"No."

"Okay."

"I will call him and see what's up, Ken said. "I'll call you back."

They both hung up the phone. Gabby called England.

"Hey girl."

"Hey, I just went by the hospital and the nurse told me that Calvin had been discharged."

"When did all of that happen?"

"Earlier today."

"That's good, isn't it?"

"I hope so," Gabby said, "but there is no cure for HIV."

"Well, we know that. He's just going to have to take his medicine."

"Okay, I'm pulling up in the driveway. I'll call you later."

"Holla."

The girls both hung up. Gabby went into the house to see what was for dinner. As she walked through the doorway, she didn't smell anything. She knew if she didn't smell the food, then her mom was not home, and she had to cook or find something to eat. Gabby walked into the kitchen and looked on the whiteboard to find that her mom had left a message. She told Gabby to pick up her brother and sister from practice and get them pizza or something. The money was in the cookie jar. Gabby wasn't too eager to pick up her siblings, but she had to. As she was going upstairs to her bedroom, her cell phone rang.

"Hello."

"Hi, Gabby this is Matthew. What's up?"

"Nothin, I am just getting in."

"Okay. You want me to call you back, or do you want to call me back once you're settled?"

"No, I can talk for a while," Gabby said. "Later I have to pick up my brother and sister from their practices and take them to get pizza."

"Cool, I can come with y'all."

"Okay, our favorite place is Benigno's."

"Great, that's mine too. I'll meet you at what time?"

"Probably about seven."

"Okay, see you then. Bye."

"Bye."

Gabby lay across her bed and fell asleep. She didn't wake up until about 6:30. She looked at the clock and jumped out of bed. It was way past the time she was supposed to pick up her siblings. She ran downstairs, grabbed her keys and purse, and ran out the door. Her phone was buzzing because calls were coming in from her sister, brother, and mom. She allowed the phone to buzz until she got on the highway. She called her brother and sister to let them know that she was on her way. She called her mom to tell her why she was running late and that she was on her way. She also had to call Matthew to let him know she was going to be late. As she drove down the street, Gabby had thoughts about Calvin. She wanted to see him and make sure he was okay. She also wondered if Ken had the virus too. He told them that he'd been tested, but Gabby was not sure that he would tell them if he did have it.

After picking up her brother and sister, she headed to Benigno's for pizza. Matthew called to tell her he was already there and would hold them a table. Although traffic was bad, she reassured him that she would be there in about 20 minutes. Then she called England to tell her that she had to take her brother and sister to Benigno's. After Gabby parked her car, she said bye to England, and they all got out and raced to the door. Gabby looked around for Matthew. She spotted him waving his hand, beckoning to them. She waved back and headed that way.

"Hi, you," said Gabby.

"Hi!"

Matthew got up, grabbed Gabby's hand and kissed her on the cheek.

"Matthew, this is my sister Nona and my brother Noel."

"Hi, Nona and Noel, please join me."

"Hi Matthew," said Nona and Noel in unison.

"Well, how was school today?"

"Good," said Nona and Noel.

"How was your day?" asked Nona.

"My day was good," said Matthew. "I finally got an opportunity to wash and clean out my car."

"What kind of car do you have?"

"It's nothin' fancy, just a Honda Civic."

"Okay, cool," said Noel.

"Okay, are we hungry, or are we starving?"

"We are starving!"

"Okay, what are we waiting for—let's order the largest pizza they have!"

"All right," said Noel!

As they waited for the waitress, they engaged in small talk. Noel and Nona wanted to know more about Matthew and how he met Gabby. Gabby was uncomfortable with some of the questions her siblings were asking, but Matthew wasn't shaking out of his boots. He held his posture and gave good eye contact while being interrogated. He answered the questions because he wanted Gabby to also know more about him. He glanced at Gabby every now and then to make sure she was paying attention. She was.

"So, Matthew, how did you meet Gabby?"

"Well, Nona, I met Gabby at a summer job we had last year."

"Do you go to Gabby's school?"

"No, I attend a school in Dekalb."

"That's far from us."

"Yes, it is," said Gabby.

"Really far," said Noel.

"How did you all manage to keep in touch?"

"That's an easy one," said Matthew. "We have each other's phone numbers and we both have cars. Every now and then we meet up with our friends for lunch or dinner. And we talk a lot over the phone."

"Have you ever been on a date with my sister by yourself?"

"No."

"Why?" inquired Nona, "Don't you find her attractive?"

Matthew looked at Gabby. He thought about her beautiful eyes, her cocoa-colored skin, and how he enjoyed looking at her lips. He thought she had the most beautifully defined lips that any girl could possibly have. Just before he started to answer the question, the server came to take the order.

"Hi, welcome to Benigno's. Sorry it took me so long to come and take your order, but as you see we're short of help this evening. Are you all ready to order?"

"Yes," said Matthew, "we would like a large supreme pizza with four Cokes. Right?".

"You are correct," said Gabby.

"Oh, can we have extra cheese?"

"Noel, you can have anything you want."

"Make that extra cheese," said Matthew.

"You got it!" said the waitress.

As soon as the waitress completed the order and walked away, the question and answer session resumed.

"Okay, where were we?"

"You were going to talk about your beloved Gabby," said Noel in a joking way.

They all laughed except Gabby. She looked at Noel in a strange way, as if she didn't approve of his joke. Noel recognized that look and sat back in his chair.

"Yes, you were asking me if Gabby and I ever went out on a date without our friends," said Matthew. "And the answer to that is no."

"Why? Don't you find her attractive?"

Gabby just sat there shaking her head and then she spoke.

"You are so nosey. Noel and Nona, you are not too far behind. Matthew and I are friends. We don't think about dating each other."

Matthew was looking at Gabby and thinking that she should only speak for herself. Matthew was very attracted to Gabby and had tried to ask her out, but the timing wasn't right, so he thought. He also knew that Gabby had been trying to hint to him that he needed to take England out. However, Matthew was interested in Gabby and had only thoughts of her.

"Matthew, just answer the questions! Gabby is a little shy."

Matthew couldn't wait to answer the question. He thought Gabby would then realize that he really liked her, not England.

"Okay, I will answer the question just for you, Noel, since you think you need to know. Your sister Gabby is very beautiful. She has eyes like a sparrow and a beautiful smile that I just adore. So, to me she is very attractive."

"If she is all that, why haven't you taken her out?" asked Nona, with an attitude.

"Well, Gabby has a very busy schedule, and I didn't want to interrupt her quest to become a pro at what she enjoys doing."

"People can make time for others if they want to," said Nona. "At least that's what my mama says."

"You are correct, Nona. People can make time for each other if they want to—"

"You should come to our house someday," interrupted Noel.

"Okay, I will when Gabby invites me."

The pizza arrived and they were ready to eat. Matthew blessed the food and served everyone a slice of pizza. Gabby observed Matthew as he took on a male role in this gathering. He reminded her of her dad, taking control and making sure everyone was being taken care of. She liked the fact that he was in control from the beginning and was enjoying it. At first, they ate in silence, enjoying the taste and aroma of the pizza. Noel broke the silence.

"This is the best pizza in the world."

"How do you know it's the best," said Nona, "if this is the only place you go for pizza?"

"Nona, you know we have frozen pizzas at home."

"Well, boy, you can't compare that to this, are you crazy?"

"Yeah, you right," said Noel. "This is fresh out the oven and has not been in a freezer for 50 years."

"It is good," proclaimed Matthew.

"I agree."

"So, Gabby, are you ready for the prom?"

"Just as ready as I'm going to be."

"Who's taking you to the prom, Gabby?" asked Noel.

Gabby looked at Noel with that weird look again. She wanted to wring his neck because she knew exactly what he was doing. Noel knew that Gabby was not dating anyone special and was probably going to the prom with England and a group of girls.

"I am going to the prom alone, if it's any of your business."

"Well, you don't have to get bent out of shape about it. The boy just asked you a question."

"Nona, you are not in this, so just continue to feed your face."

"Yes, ma'am."

"Hey, Gabby," said Matthew. "I would like to go to your prom if you invite me, and you can come to mine. I don't have a date either."

He is good looking and fine, Gabby thought. She imagined he would probably turn a lot of heads as soon as they walked through the door. Yeah, this would be awesome.

"Well, okay, that sounds like a plan, said Gabby. "Now when is your prom?"

"The week after yours."

"Wow! I guess I need to go shopping for a dress."

"You have plenty of nice dresses already," said Noel. "Why buy another one?"

"Boy, don't you know anything," said Nona. "That's what women do. They shop and shop. Now she has an excuse to shop."

"If I was your dad," retorted Noel, "I wouldn't let you spend up my money like that."

"But you ain't daddy," shouted Nona.

Matthew laughed at the way Nona talked to Noel. She was so country and cute, thought Matthew. As he listened to Nona and Noel go back and forth with their thoughts and opinions, he glanced at Gabby and smiled. Gabby looked at him and shook her head with a smile.

On the way home, Gabby thought she needed to make sure that her brother and sister knew that she and Matthew were just friends. She knew that as soon as they got home, they were going to tell their parents about the date and exaggerate the story. Matthew was a very bright boy and had made a way for himself. No, his parents weren't financially secure like Gabby's parents, but Gabby was very fond of Matthew and believed that he would be a success in life. Just because a person grew up without some of the finer things in life, she thought, it didn't mean he was poor. She knew that one day he would be much better off than his parents.

Chapter 15

England

E ngland was at the table completing her homework, when a commercial came on about a seminar for students on their way to college. It appeared that the seminar was going to be split up into several mini workshops. Each workshop addressed one aspect of a freshman's life on campus. The commercial named the website where you could receive more detailed information about the seminar.

England wrote the website down and ran to the next room to get on the computer. On the site, one of the presenters was a female doctor who would talk about sex, HIV/AIDS and how to stay healthy as a college student. There were more workshops on good topics, such as credit card usage and how not to get into debt at an early age; how to build good study habits; how to balance activities and classwork; and how to maneuver around a campus in a safe way. England thought this would be a great outing for Gabby, Nikki, and her to attend. Nikki really needed to go because she could get more information about where to go to take an HIV test so that she could know her status. As long as she didn't know her status, she would have sleepless nights and difficult days trying to stay focused. Being in Nikki's situation was a nightmare.

England called Gabby right away.

"Hello."
"Hello, Gabby, what's going on?"

"Nothin' much, I'm just getting in from dance practice," Gabby said. "What's up on your end, have you heard from Nikki?"

"No, but I just heard about a seminar that they are having here for upcoming freshmen."

"Okay, tell me more."

"Well, this seminar is broken down into mini-workshops. Each workshop will focus on a component of life on a college campus."

"Okay."

"One of the workshops is talking about HIV and AIDS and how to stay healthy," England continued. "My first thought when I heard the commercial was, if we can get Nikki to attend, maybe she'll see how important it is for her to get tested. What you think?"

"Well, it's good that you want to help her," Gabby responded. "I think it's a good idea. But she will still have to decide if and when she wants to know her status."

"Yeah, you're right," said England, "but she must realize that it is worse not knowing than to know."

"If she comes out in the clear," said Gabby, "she must still continue to be tested. Although that will get her heartbeat throbbing, she must continue to be tested every six months, at least for a while."

"But it's still better to know than not to know," said England.

"So, when is the seminar--what time, and how much?"

"It is this weekend at 9:00 a.m. and the cost is $25.00 which includes freebees and lunch."

"That's not bad," said Gabby. "I guess we can go online to register, if it's not too late?"

"No, I think we can register and pick up the tickets at Will Call."

"Do you still want to go if Nikki doesn't go?"

"Yes," said England. "I think there's going to be a wealth of information that we'll need later on. We can always go back and access it if we need it."

"Okay, I will register for it tonight."

"Alright, I'm going to call Nikki and see if she'd like to go with us."

"Okay, England, I'll see you tomorrow."

England hung up and dialed Nikki's number.

"Hello, Nikki, this is England."

"Hey, England, I was just getting ready to call you!"

"Okay, what's up?"

"A friend of mine was telling me about this workshop for upcoming freshmen," said Nikki. "I was going to go to the website to check it out. Then I was going to call you and give you more information about it, to see if you and Gabby would want to attend."

"We were thinking alike. I had just seen the commercial and I was going to call you and see if you wanted to go."

"Well, I guess it's a done deal. No need to go to the website."

"No, you don't have to check it out now," said England, "now that you've heard it from two incredibly reliable sources."

"I guess you're right."

"How is school coming along?"

"It's good," said Nikki. "I just cannot wait until graduation. I'm ready to go off to college."

"Well, it won't be long."

"No, I'll be finished with all of my required courses come January," said Nikki. "Then I will take one college course. I guess something like English or Algebra."

"That's good, girl," said England. "You are on a roll."

"Yeah, what about you?"

"I'll have to do my whole senior year. However, I only need two classes come January. I'll be going home around noon time."

"That's good," said Nikki. "Hey, I need to thank you for all of your support. I'm still trying to deal with my situation and Calvin."

"Have you spoken to Calvin?"

"No. Every time I call, he is either asleep or not at home."

"Has he tried to contact you?" asked England.

"No."

"Nikki, don't you think you need to take an HIV test now?"

"Yes, I've been thinking about it, but I am so afraid."

"I understand your fear," said England, "but there is a possibility that you are okay, and you need to verify that. And if something is wrong, you can get treatments in the early stages and live a long and prosperous life."

"It's the fear of not knowing. And since I don't know, I'm not sleeping very well."

"It's better to know, so you'll be sure what you're dealing with. Have you talked with your mom or anybody else?"

"No, but my mom has been asking about Calvin," Nikki said. "She thought Calvin was a genius. Calvin's got those eyes, and he knew how to look innocent."

"I know what you mean. But have you tried going to his house?"

"No, I really don't want to see him. I'm just so embarrassed about all of this. How do you keep it all together, England?"

"Well, it's not easy. I dated a couple of times, and the boys just wanted a sexual relationship. I never met anyone who just wanted to have a sexless relationship if there is such a thing. I think staying grounded in the Lord kept me on my path. I am a member of our youth department and growing up I was always busy doing church activities. Our Youth Minister always talked about having relationships at our age. They brought in all kinds of speakers and vocal artists to help get the message across. I guess I paid attention to what was being said."

"England, you are blessed to have such a good church that focused on the youth. Most parents don't even talk to us about sex, or anything related to it."

"Well, some parents are so uncomfortable with the subject," England replied. "They don't know how to talk about sex or much of anything else. They may ask you about your grades, but they are not checking up on you at school and they are not asking too many questions about your friends."

"I know my parents are busy focusing on their careers," said Nikki. "And when they do get home, they are so tired they just want to eat and go to sleep. It's the same thing day in and day out. Then before you know it—it's the weekend."

"Nikki, if you want me to go to the doctor with you, I will. I'll be there for you. Just let me know when you want to go."

"Thanks, England. You're such a good person. I wish I'd met you before I ran into Calvin. I probably would not be in this predicament."

"Well, you know me now. So don't hesitate to call."

"Okay, girl, I'll talk to you on Saturday. I need to go study."

"Okay, see you then. Bye."

England felt pretty good after she hung up the phone with Nikki. She actually thought it was a relief. She was glad that Nikki's friend extended the invitation and Nikki decided to go. Just maybe Nikki would see how important it was for her to be tested and find out her status. England was hoping that Nikki didn't go to the website to get more information, because the information might make her uncomfortable and change her mind. England also had thoughts about Calvin. She was wondering if they would ever see him again. Would he come back to school? She was quite puzzled. England was headed back to the kitchen when she heard the doorbell ring.

"I'll get it, Mom!"

"Okay!"

England rushed to the door to open it. Ken was standing there, and England invited him in.

"It's Ken, Mom!"

"Okay. Hi, Ken."

"Hi! How are you?"

"Great! But I'll feel much better when I finish grading these papers."

"Teaching little ones is a job, huh?" replied Ken.

"Yes, you got that right!"

England and Ken headed into the kitchen.

"What's up, England?"

"Nothing, and you?"

"Well, I just thought I would come talk with you. Are you too busy?"

"No, I was just completing some calculus problems."

"Well, I can do those for you. How many do you have left to do?"

"Just two."

"Okay, I will do one and you can do the other."

"Sounds like a deal to me."

England and Ken sat at the table and started working on the problems. While England was working her problem, she wondered why Ken was at her house during a weeknight. Throughout the week they didn't have time to visit because their Advance Placement classes gave them more than enough homework to keep them busy all evening long. Ken must have something on his mind, England thought, to come by here tonight. They worked in silence, so quiet you could hear a pin drop. England's cell phone rang.

"Hello."

"Hey, girl, did you finish that last math problem?" asked Gabby.

"Not yet."

"Are you working on it?"

"Well, actually Ken is working that one for me."

"What! Why is he over there on a weeknight?"

"That, I can't answer yet?"

"What do you mean, you can't answer it?" Gabby asked. "Is he looking in your mouth?"

"Uh huh."

"Okay, you can't talk now. Tell him I said hello. But why is he even there?"

"Gabby, I will call you back."

"Girl, you better call me back. Don't go to sleep before calling me. I am going to wait up for your call."

"Bye Gabby."

"Bye!"

England looked at Ken and started working her problem again. She forgot to tell Ken that Gabby said hello.

"Tell Gabby she talks too loud. I heard her every word."

"Whaaat! You did?"

"Yeah."

"So, you heard her when she said tell you hello?"

"Uh huh."

"Okay, I'm finished with this one. What about you?"

"Oh, I've been finished. I was just double checking."

"You are too smart," said England. "A lot of book sense."

"Okay, what does that mean?" Ken asked.

"Nothing, you're just smart. So, what's up?"

"England, I have been a real jerk. I know through the years that I have hurt a lot of people, including you and Gabby. I just want to apologize for my behavior. As I look back on my actions, I didn't have a clue about what could happen as a result of my promiscuous behavior. I just thought I was having fun and doing what boys my age do. It just made life a little better. At least that's what I thought. I became so cocky with it. I was certain I was doing the right thing. Girls were not complaining and not too many said no. The ones who said no, I just moved on. I didn't think anything was wrong with that."

"And now you have finally come to your senses," England said, "and realize that you were playing a dangerous game?"

"Well, I wouldn't say it's dangerous."

"What would you call it then?"

"I thought I was just being inconsiderate of others, but that's not true. I didn't take anything from anyone. I just had sex."

"Why now? Why are you looking at this now?"

"Calvin."

"Yes, there's Calvin. Calvin and you were waiting for something to happen. You had warning after warning. But you thought you could continue to have sex without any consequences."

"Well, I used condoms," Ken said.

"Condoms sometimes don't work. They are man-made, are they not?"

"Yeah! But I never had anything to go wrong."

"So, you think," said England. "But your boy did."

Silence filled the room.

"Well, look at it this way, Ken. The worst case scenario is that you may become HIV positive later on down the road. We don't know. Do you know the statistics of black men contracting HIV? Better yet, do you know how many black children and teens have been diagnosed with HIV or AIDS?"

"No, England, I don't."

"My dad told me out of all the children and teens that have been diagnosed, about 60 to 70% are black children and youth."

"What! That's high."

"Yes, it is. But it's true and we have no control over it. I'm not saying that all of these kids contracted the disease through sex, but I am saying that the number is creeping up every day. As a black woman I will have to be very careful, because black women are 20 times more likely to become infected than other racial groups."

"Wow! So, I have a better chance of contracting it than any other male from another race?"

"According to statistics you do."

Silence once again filled the room.

"You know," said England, "I think something like this had to happen for God to get your attention. I'm sorry that this happened to Calvin, and I really hope he pulls through it."

"Well, I don't blame God," said Ken. "I blame myself and Calvin. We were out there running wild and having fun. We weren't thinking and, if we did, our thoughts didn't stay long, especially if it was something that we really wanted to do."

"So, what now?"

"For me, I'm just going to pray and ask God to forgive me for disappointing Him," said Ken. "I have had several meetings with our pastor as well as a counselor to help me deal with my frustrations, and I blame myself for Calvin's condition. I'm just trying to get by on a daily basis. Trying not to answer any questions related to Calvin. I know it seems like he has fallen off the face of the earth, because we didn't have any warning of his situation. I'm sure people know something, but are just not saying anything around me."

"You heard what that girl said… What's her name?"

"Oh yeah, you're talking about Erica."

"Yeah! That's her name! Erica has a big mouth," said Ken. "Always has and always will. She doesn't know anything."

"Oh, okay."

"Well, England, it's getting late, and we do have school tomorrow. I'll see you at school."

"Okay, let me walk you to the door."

They both said their goodbyes once again. England ran right upstairs. She was too tired to call Gabby. She knew they would stay on the phone much longer than she really wanted to. So, she just took her shower, said her prayers, and got in bed.

However, she couldn't sleep because she was thinking about Ken. She thought he was smart, and he had a bright future, if he lived to see it. She was frightened for him. She also knew that all things were in God's hand. He had the last decision on anything and everything.

Chapter 16

Gabby and England

Gabby and England decided that they would go and visit Calvin after school. Calvin had been homebound since he went to the hospital. The gossip about him was really low key. No one knew how many girlfriends Calvin really had. Most of the girls in the senior and junior class were walking on pins and needles. Other than that, nothing much was going on.

Basketball season was over and now it is time for the prom. Everyone was excited. The year had gone by so quickly and summer was close by. Conversation filled the air about summer jobs, summer classes at certain colleges, volunteer work, and just getting that last minute free time before the first year of college.

Gabby and England were at the lockers when China approached them. She walked right up to them and started talking.

"Hi, Gabby and England."

They were so stunned the two girls couldn't say anything at first. They looked at each other to make sure they both heard China speaking to them.

"Hi, China," said Gabby.

England didn't reply. She just stared at China. China looked at England, waiting for England to speak. England looked behind her to make sure her clique wasn't preparing to jump them.

"What's on your mind, China?" asked England.

"Well, I just wanted to let both of you know that I really never did like you. I figured y'all thought you were better than everyone else. But you really don't think that. Y'all just don't get in everybody's business. You mainly stay to yourselves. You don't have many boys running after you. The ones you had you didn't keep, because y'all just couldn't get into the swing of things. Y'all had some good looking guys wanting to date you, but y'all just didn't fit into our seam. Y'all are different, but what makes y'all different?"

"China, we are different but yet we're the same," said Gabby.

"Yeah, we're different because we believe that sex can hurt more than help you," said England. "And we believe that we are the same because we are females probably around the same age and we're fairly well known. However, we're known for different reasons. Just to give you an example, I am known as a cheerleader, a girl with high values, and a student with a grade point average of 3.8. Gabby is known for her ability to keep up with all of her extracurricular activities and her 3.9 grade point average. And you, China, let me see. Umm, what are you good at that everybody knows about?"

Gabby looked at England, because she knew that England was getting ready to get China fired up and angry. Here it comes.

"China, do you even have a grade point average? Do you even know what that is? No, I didn't think so. So, China, what are you good for? I don't know, so tell me. Or should I go ask Dominique, Peter, Devin? Or maybe I could just go ask Mays. What do you think?"

"England, you are such a dirt bag," China shot back. "I should put your head through that locker."

"Well, bring it," retorted England, "if you think you are bad enough to complete that task all by yourself, Ms. Tramp."

"Okay, no one is going to put anyone anywhere," said Gabby. "China, what is it that you really want?"

"I really want to kick England's butt."

"Like I said, bring it on!"

Gabby got between the two girls. As she did, a teacher observed the commotion and walked over to ask the girls if there was a problem. The girls shook their heads. England and China backed away from each other. England started to mumble under her breath and walk away.

"China, you're going to have to stop trying to get stuff started," said Gabby. "You need to be thinking about finishing school and moving forward in your life, not trying to see if you can get us in trouble by inviting people to fight you. I know the game you're playing, and you don't get to me at all. But, England, on the other hand, if you keep pushing her, she might not be able to control herself. So, if I were you, I would back off and go spend my time somewhere else. Put your time and energy into something of importance. Stop focusing on us."

"Call it how you want it," China shot back. "This is not over. I am tired of England thinking she can run me."

"How can she run you," Gabby said, "when she doesn't even speak or talk to you?"

"She doesn't have to open her mouth. It's the way she looks at me."

"Well, stop looking at her and maybe you won't notice her looking at you."

"I just don't like her or you," said China.

"Again, move on and stop focusing on us. We don't need or want your attention."

China rolled her eyes and walked away from Gabby. Gabby walked down the hallway and out the door. She saw England sitting on the bench waiting for her.

"What took you so long?" England said. "I started to leave you."

"Girl, you know you weren't going to leave me."

"All right, don't be too sure of yourself."

"England, you're going to have to stop letting China get to you. She knows she can get you to react to her foolishness."

"I can't stand that girl with her dumb behind," England said.

"Don't say that, because she just might have an intellectual disability."

"There's nothing wrong with that girl. She just wants attention. Besides, she is bored right about now because she doesn't have anyone else to sleep with."

"You don't think she's trying to pick on you?" asked Gabby.

"Oh! You are so not right!"

The girls started laughing and walked to the car. England pulled out of the parking lot and started driving towards Atlanta Highway. As the girls rode, they listened to the radio. Every time one of their favorite songs came on, they would pump up the volume and sing with the artist. England turned into Calvin's subdivision. Gabby cut the music down and started talking to England.

"Maybe we should have called."

"We can still call, but we will be in his driveway."

Gabby called Calvin's number. The phone rang several times before someone answered.

"Hello."

"Hello, this is Gabby, and I wanted to know if it was okay to stop by and see Calvin."

"Yes, Gabby, that would be great. He hasn't had much company since he got home from the hospital."

"Okay, we're in your driveway."

"Well, come on in."

Gabby flipped her phone shut and placed it back into her purse. She realized that it had been a while since they'd seen Calvin. She had mixed feelings and started to get nervous. The palms of her hands started to get a little moist. England was feeling the same. She thought Gabby's thoughts as well. She hoped that Calvin would like to see them as much as Gabby wanted to see and talk to him.

Gabby rang the doorbell and Calvin's mother came to the door.

"Hello, you two."

"Hi, how are you?"

"I am doing fine."

"That's good to hear," said England.

"Calvin is looking forward to seeing you guys. I told him you had called several times, trying to come and visit with him. So, he's waiting. Gabby, you know your way, so go on up."

"Yes, ma'am."

Gabby and England walked up the steps and turned the corner to go to Calvin's bedroom. As they entered, they were shocked to see such a frail body. Calvin had lost a great deal of weight and his cheeks were sunken in. They both tried to keep their composure.

"Hello, Calvin," they said in unison.

"Hey, what's up?"

"Nothing, we just finished up our classes and decided to pay you a visit."

"Well, thanks for coming by."

"How are the homebound classes going?"

"I guess they're going well. I try to do as much as I can. I'm on so much medicine, sometimes I just can't get up."

"I'm glad to hear that you're taking your medicine."

"Guess who came over to see me?"

"Who?"

"Guess, England. It's someone I've always wanted to see."

"Oh yeah, your dad."

"Yep!" said Calvin. "It took this for him to come and see me, spend time with me."

"Well, at least you were able to spend time with him," said England.

"But I didn't want to spend time with him. It's too late for us to be anything."

"Well Calvin, you must forgive him for not being there for you. You can't hold a grudge forever."

"I was fine not knowing he was still here in Atlanta. I was doing well not knowing. It seems he just brought some pain with him, dropped it off, and left."

"Yeah, oh well, at least you know what he looks like now."

"My mom called him. Don't ask me why he came. He didn't come when she called him before, which was a lot of times."

"So, Calvin, have you been able to tell your partners about your situation?"

"Not as many as I'd like."

"What does that mean?"

"Just what I said, England. I haven't been able to really have phone conversations. And the doctors told my mom not to let people visit with me until my immune system gets closer to normal."

"Have you spoken to Nikki?"

"No, but I've made a list of people I need to contact. I will, but slowly. She's on the list."

Calvin became drowsy as he talked and was dozing off and on. He had a lot of medicine to take. He has some good days and bad days. His main goal was to try to build up his immune system.

"So, what have y'all been up to?"

"Nothing much. We're getting ready for prom, then graduation."

"Do you think you're going to make it to graduation?" England asked.

"Probably not, even if I feel better," said Calvin. "I just don't want to go."

"When was the last time you talked with Ken?"

"I saw Ken two days ago. He came over for a while."

"Calvin, is it okay that we say a prayer before we leave? We know you need your rest."

"No prayers, the preacher has come and gone," replied Calvin. "I know that my behavior justifies this situation I'm in. However, I do need to know how I got it—who passed it to me."

"I'm sure you'll think about it when you get enough strength to stay up for longer periods of time."

"Yep."

"Well, Calvin, I guess we better be going. See you later."

"Bye England."

England walked out of the room and down the hallway towards the staircase.

"Calvin, take care of yourself and make sure you do what the doctors tell you."

"Gabby, thanks for being so strong. You know, I really wanted you to be one of my girlfriends, and I am so glad that you didn't go too far with me. I wish more girls would have said no."

Calvin looked at the ceiling.

"Gabby, I have full blown AIDS now, and I don't know how long I'm going to live."

"Oh my God, I am so sorry. Does Ken know this?"

"No, just my mom, my doctors, and now you."

"Oh, Calvin, I am so sorry."

"Not as sorry as me."

Gabby walked out of the room with more weight on her heart. She went down the stairs very slowly. By the time she was at the bottom, both England and Calvin's mom were staring at her. Calvin's mom knew he had told her about his condition. The look on Gabby's face told the story. Calvin's mom didn't say anything. She thanked the girls for coming by and told them she hoped to see them soon. The girls said goodbye, walked out the house and got into the car. The ride home was very subdued. Then England spoke.

"Gabby, what do you imagine he thinks about day in and day out?"

"He's probably thinking about why he wasn't safer. Why he didn't get in the habit of using a condom on a regular basis."

"You don't think he has any regrets for having sex at this time in his life?"

"Of course not," Gabby said, "I know he wishes he would have been more careful."

"I believe he's probably thinking he should have just stayed at the level of kissing and groping," England replied.

"That's the way it gets started. All of that kissing and touching just make your hormones scream for more. Before you know it, things have gotten heated, and you lose all control. Do you feel me?"

"Yeah," England said. "I've been there to a certain point, may I say. It gets scary too."

"Uh huh! A kiss and hug tonight; the next date you take it a little further."

"I am so glad, Gabby, that you didn't give in to him. That could've been you in the same situation. Look at Nikki. Poor Nikki. She has a lot to lose."

"I didn't like him like you like Ken," Gabby said. "I thought I had to worry about you keeping it together."

"I guess I haven't been fooling you at all."

"No."

"I just didn't know what to do," said England. "I like him, and I know he likes me. But he has had so many girlfriends. Now he just looks aggressive in a dirty way."

"I think he's always liked you," Gabby said. "He just got caught up into the game. He had to make sure the boys didn't call him out, so he dated girls that he knew he could report back to his clan."

"I know we said it all the time, but do you think they really shared that much of their business like that."

"England, that's not business. That's being proud of the fact that you scored."

"Well, all of them in that clique need to come and take a hard look at Calvin. I know it would put an end to some of their promiscuous behavior."

"I'm sure some of them will think they were not all that smart or clever," said Gabby. "Some won't care. They'll continue with their behaviors because they feel like they cannot be touched. They will still think that AIDS is for certain people only."

"Gabby, I'm afraid of going to college."

"Why, England?"

"They say college campuses are loaded with HIV cases."

"I know," said Gabby, "but that doesn't mean you have to be in the number. You can have an awesome college experience without getting HIV or any other diseases, if you do the right thing."

"How do I do the right thing?" asked England.

"You just don't date boys who are flaunting it."

"What! I'm supposed to date some ugly boy or a nerd?"

"I didn't say all that," said Gabby. "Just make sure they're not after your body."

"Suppose I think I won't like the person, but he ends up being the perfect sex machine?"

"Dump him while you still can."

"Girl, you sound like me," said England.

"I truly don't want to be you."

"You got a problem with me?"

"No, England, you just get feisty too easily."

"So, what are you saying, I need anger management?"

"No," said Gabby, "you just put a person in check without thinking."

"Well, check this out," replied England, pulling into Gabby's driveway, "Get out my car!"

"You mean your momma's car!"

Gabby got out and slammed the door.

"Don't slam my door unless you want a beat down!"

Gabby walked to the front door.

"Go home, England, and call me when you get home!"

"I don't have to call you; you are not my mom!"

England pulled away.

Chapter 17

Gabby and England

It was Saturday morning and England's alarm clock went off. As she rose, her TV came on startling her. England had set the timer the night before so she could get up and get moving. She felt solemn as she dragged herself to the bathroom to take her shower.

England's mom was downstairs making breakfast. She was so excited about England going to the summit for upcoming college students. She was going to take her and Gabby. She didn't trust England's driving in the fast-paced traffic near the downtown area.

Still a little drowsy, England went downstairs to the kitchen and poured some smoothie that her mom had blended. After taking a swallow England gagged.

"Mom!"

"What is it, girl!"

"What is this? Is it even palatable?"

"Yes, it will give your day a jump start. It'll boost up your energy level."

"Gabby's dog wouldn't like this, and he eats anything. What else did you cook?"

"Eggs, toast, and turkey bacon."

"Thanks, I think I'll eat that."

The doorbell rang and England's dad, Mr. Desto, answered the door. Gabby and her dad were on the doorstep.

"Good morning, come on in. How's it going, Mr. McWright?"

"Hey, all is good. What about you?"

"I am doing fine. And you Gabby?"

"I'm good."

"Well, come on in and have some breakfast."

No," said Mr. McWright. "I'm going to wait and eat breakfast with my old lady."

While the men were sitting and chatting about their careers, Gabby headed to the kitchen to grab something to eat.

"Good morning."

"Good morning, Gabby," answered Mrs. Desto and England in unison.

"Gabby, have some breakfast."

"I think I will, Mrs. Desto."

"You kept me up last night."

"Is that why your eyes are puffy?" asked Gabby.

"Probably so but hurry up and fix your egg sandwich so we can go," said England.

"Where are the paper cups?"

"In the bottom of the pantry."

"What do you have to drink?"

"Check the fridge, just don't drink that stuff in the blender."

"Why?"

England whispered, "It's nasty."

England looked at Gabby and laughed. She tried it anyway and started gagging.

England's mom came into the kitchen.

"What's wrong, Gabby?"

"Mmm, I must have choked."

England started laughing. She was waiting to see if Gabby was going to tell her mom the truth. Gabby looked at England and just tried to play it off, pretending she was choking on her water.

"Nothing, ma'am."

"Are you sure? I thought I heard you in here gagging."

"I just got choked on some water."

"Okay, are you girls ready?"

"Yes, Mom."

The three of them walked out and got into the car. England sat in the back seat and Gabby rode in the front. They always traded places when they were riding with each other's moms. This allowed each mom to bond with her daughter's best friend. The girls and the moms both enjoyed the arrangement. Gabby and Mrs. Desto were in conversation while England took a nap.

"Mrs. Desto, what will you be doing while were at the seminar?"

"I thought I would go do a half day massage and check out some sales."

"Wow! That sounds good," said Gabby. "I should have made plans to go with you instead of going to the seminar."

"Well, you're going to receive a lot of information at the seminar. This is something they do every year. The information will come in handy. You'll see."

"Yes, I guess I can obtain more information on certain things. Although I think I know all that I need to know for college living."

"You'll see, there's always something in a seminar that will be useful later on in life," said Mrs. Desto. "You may be able to put some of the information to use before you step foot on a college campus."

"Perhaps."

"Gabby, you are a straight "A" student. How have you been able to balance school, extracurricular activities, dating, and family time?"

"Well, I keep a calendar. It's like my soul mate. I have to write everything in it so I won't schedule things on top of each other. First, I look at my activities. They include my Christian organization, Bible study, cheerleading, and dance. I look at my advanced classes and determine how much time I'll need to study. I first mark on the calendar those hours I'm going to use for studying. I work around those hours to plan other activities. It takes about two to three weeks to get a schedule to flow right. I have a busy schedule, but I like being busy. It probably has saved me plenty of times."

"What do you mean?"

"Well, so much is happening with teenagers our age. Some girls are getting pregnant, some are getting their hearts broken, which may affect their relationship with men later on, some are getting diseases that they can't get rid of, and some are experiencing living as gay people."

"You're correct," said Mrs. Desto. "Year after year teenagers are acting more like adults and living adult lives, without the necessary equipment to survive. Some children, adolescents, and teenagers are asking to be adults, and some are pressured into adult acts. There's a gap between our parenting techniques, and what kids see on TV and hear on the radio. You have some parents who try to raise their children right, but they're competing against Satan. Even if a child watches good channels, you have these crazy commercials that come on with the actors half naked. Moreover, kids will get all kinds of information from their buddies. Some kids will act on the information; others will not."

"Mrs. Desto, those kids who act on the information will start a link that breaks away from the chain. Once one link is broken, others fall prey."

"Yes, there are so many children that are in situations they don't have to be in. If only they'd stood strong, just said 'no' or walked away."

"So many young lives are lost just because a child did not make the right decision," agreed Gabby.

England woke up from her nap wanting to break into the conversation.

"What are you two talking about?"

"Oh, we're just talking about how people, or should I say teenagers, make decisions that can destroy their lives," said Gabby.

"Who made a decision that destroyed her life?"

"No particular person. We were just talking about the youth in this world and how they're viewing things," Gabby replied.

"But we do know of some kids at our school," said England, "who are battling STDs and emotional depression."

Mrs. Desto cut in.

"Okay, girls, looks like we made it. I will drop you off right here. Call me when you're finished. On the way home we finish our conversation."

"Okay, Mom, we'll see you later. Have fun and I love ya."

"I love you girls, too. Bye."

The girls headed to the door, while England rummaged through her purse looking for the tickets. As they got closer to the door, Gabby spotted Nikki and her friend. Gabby was waving her hand, while at the same time telling England that she saw Nikki. Gabby pulled England by the shirt to guide her, while she looked for the tickets. Gabby and Nikki were heading toward each other, still waving.

"Hi, Gabby and England."

"Hi," the girls said in unison.

Nikki said, "This is my friend, Tracey. We attend the same school."

"Hi, Tracy."

"Hi, it's nice to meet the both of you. I've heard so much about you--especially you, England."

"I hope it was all good."

"Yeah, it was," said Tracy.

"Good, because I hate to fight when I know I am looking good," replied England.

"Oh girl, what did you come out here for?"

"I'm looking for my future husband."

"Oh yeah, I guess we'll help you do just that."

"England, you found our tickets yet?"

"Yeah girl, I had you scared for a minute, didn't I?"

"No. I know you're organized," said Gabby. "Besides, you were the one to buy the tickets. So, I knew you were on point. You just need to clean out that junky purse of yours."

"Not as junky as yours."

"Please, let's go."

The girls didn't anticipate the long line. They thought most teenagers would still be in bed this time of morning. As the girls observed the crowd and checked out the other kids, England was wondering if Nikki knew about the workshop that was going to discuss potential health risks on the college campuses. Would Nikki use this information to motivate her to take a blood test immediately. As they got closer to the door, a young lady moved toward them passing out brochures. The brochure read, "How to Live and Survive on a College Campus."

They all opened the brochure to see what it was about. It was the schedule of the different workshops, their times and their locations. It was easy to read and well put together.

As England skimmed through the brochure in search of the health workshop, Gabby elbowed her to get her attention and pointed to it.

Tracy spoke up, "I suggest we first go to the workshops that are only offered once."

The girls didn't reply right away. They were still looking at the entire brochure.

"Yes, it appears some workshops are being offered more times than others," said England, "I agree with you, Tracy."

"Okay, so let's start putting the workshops in the order we would like to attend them."

"Okay."

By the time the girls put the workshops in order, they were at the door going in. The last workshop on the list was the health workshop. England suggested that they go to it last. She, out of all of them, knew that part of the workshop would focus on HIV/AIDS. She'd researched this particular workshop thoroughly, knowing that the information was going to be overwhelming, but it was going to educate them to the fullest and definitely be worthwhile.

The girls moved into the first workshop, searching for four seats together. The room was rather crowded with potential college students. The speaker was a young African American male who discussed how to balance classes and extracurricular events, such as Greek parties and athletic activities. He was a senior at Hampton University, and he viewed campus life through the eyes of a male. He started his talk with a personal story. He was able to keep the attendees' attention by being truthful and sharing his personal experiences. The girls left this workshop in high spirits. As they walked to the next workshop, they discussed the first workshop.

"Now, that was a good workshop to start with."

"Yes, but I don't think I could share all of that information with strangers."

"Well, Tracy, just imagine if he thought like you. We wouldn't have gotten this information in the context that we did. He lived through it and was able to tell about it."

"I agree with England," said Nikki. "If it were not for people like that telling their stories, we wouldn't receive firsthand information."

"'m sure it was a wake-up call, proclaimed Gabby, "and this is why he was able to stay focused on his education and cease the partying."

"Wow, college life is going to be a challenge!" said England excitedly.

"No, it will only be that way if you let the campus activities take control," said Gabby, gazing at the brochure.

"Yeah, just like he said, we will need to balance," Tracey added, "making sure we stay on top of our studies by going to class and turning in assignments on time."

The next workshop was about safety. The girls were able to get into the room and claim seats in the front row. The presenters were a college campus officer from Georgia State and someone from Student Affairs. Their presentation was about being safe on-campus. The officer told the students to make sure they made curfew at college. He also informed them to make sure to travel in pairs or quads. Campus life could be dangerous if you didn't know the safety rules. Students had to be aware of their surroundings and stay alert, especially at night while walking across campus. A lot of students stayed in the library until closing. If that was going to be the case, he told them to just be cautious and make sure they observed what was around them. He wasn't trying to instill fear in the students, but he wanted them just to be aware, be alert, and be cautious about their surroundings.

The representative from student affairs told the students to be careful with their personal information, such as Social Security numbers, addresses, and driver's license numbers. He suggested that students should talk to their parents before completing an application to get a credit card. If they got a credit card application at a kiosk located on campus, he suggested that they do not complete the application there. They should take it with them and complete it in a more private place, like their dorm room. However, he said it would be wiser to go to the bank, complete the form and give it to a bank attendant. Identity theft was very high on some campuses.

The workshops were going well. The girls were glad that they'd made the decision to attend the seminar. They had a strong desire to make their college experience as rewarding as possible. Tracy looked at her watch to see how close it was to lunch. They checked the schedule to see when the next workshop would start. With lunch time fast approaching, the girls headed to the food court.

"How did these workshops make me hungry?" said Nikki.

England agreed. "Boy, there are a lot of different types of food. I think I'm going to look around and then decide what I want."

"I already know what I want—fish and chips!" shouted England.

After finding a table, the girls went their separate ways. While in line, a young man struck up a conversation with England.

"Boy, this line is long."

"Yes, it is, but all the lines are like this."

"True. I didn't think so many people would show up for this."

"Yes, I was surprised about the crowd too."

"Sorry, I didn't introduce myself. My name is Jay, and I'll be attending ASU on an academic and football scholarship."

"Nice. My name is England, and I also will be attending ASU on an academic scholarship."

"Wow! This is a small world. That's great! Now I know somebody else who's going down there. We must exchange cell phone numbers so we can stay in touch."

"Well, aren't you going to freshman orientation?"

"No, I've had my orientation already. I'll be at football practice while you're in orientation. Actually, I'll be there way before you get there."

"Oh, I didn't know football players had to be there so much earlier than the other students."

The cashier greeted England.

"Hi, may I take your order?"

"Yes, I'd like fish and chips with a Coke."

"And you, Sir?"

"Oh, our order is not together," said England.

"It's okay, I got you, England. I would like to have the wings platter with a large, iced tea."

"That's thirteen dollars."

"You don't have to pay for my meal," said England. "I have money."

"Not a problem, England. You can pay me back when we get on the yard, and I don't have any money."

"The yard?"

"Yeah, you know, that's what they call the campus."

"How do you know that?"

"When I went to ASU, the football players were referring to the campus as 'the yard.' They also called a certain part of it 'the square.'"

"Well, okay, I'll pay you back when we get on the yard."

"Cool."

"Come and join us for lunch," England continued. "I'm sure we can pull up another chair."

"You sure your friends won't mind?"

"No, they won't."

England and Jay started walking toward the eating area. As they maneuvered their way through the crowd, someone called Jay's name. Jay looked up and saw one of his friends. He introduced England to him, and then told him he was going to go eat and he would catch up with him later. The friend nodded his head. England and Jay reached the table where Gabby, Nikki, and Tracy were already seated and eating.

"Girl, what took you so long?" shouted Nikki.

"The lines were long. This is Jay. I met him in line, and he will be attending ASU."

"Hi!" the girls said in unison.

"Hi, it's nice to meet all of you."

"So, you look like a football player. Will you be playing football by chance?"

"Yes, I'm a wide receiver."

"Wow, you must be pretty good."

"I guess."

"Did you get a football scholarship?" asked Nikki.

"Yes."

"Girl, now what did you expect?"

The girls looked at Tracy.

"That is not all he got."

"What do you mean, England? What else could have been offered to him?" said Tracy in a snobby way.

England rolled her eyes while Gabby looked on.

"For your information, Ms. Tracy, he received a full academic scholarship."

Tracy almost choked on her hamburger. Nikki put a cup of water to Tracy's mouth. She snatched the water out of Nikki's hand and rolled her eyes. Nikki had a vicious grin on her face. England and Gabby watched in suspense.

"So, what's your GPA?"

"I think I need to ask you, what's your GPA?"

"I am proud to say I have a 3.8."

"That's flattering.

Tracy stuck her chest out in a dignified way and Jay waved his hand dismissively, "So what? I have a 4.0 GPA."

"Wow!" they all said in unison.

"That's remarkable," proclaimed Gabby.

England started blushing. "Yeah, you did all of that while playing football?"

"England, I play four different sports."

He had all of their attention then.

"What are they?"

"In addition to playing football, I am on the wrestling team, track team, and baseball team."

Jay was counting on his fingers while he talked.

"But your favorite is football?"

"No, not really, I like baseball too. I think I'm going to try to walk-on the baseball team when I get to ASU."

"You're going to be busy."

"Yes, I figured playing sports will keep me grounded and out of trouble."

"Well, we'll be cheering for football and basketball seasons," said England.

"We? We who?" responded Jay.

"Oh I didn't tell you? Gabby will also be attending ASU."

"Okay, I'll have a lot of home girls on the yard."

"On the yard?" said Gabby, Nikki, and Tracy in unison.

"Yeah! That's what they call it," said England.

"The yard! I guess I can get used to that," responded Gabby.

Lunchtime was over and it was time for their next session. The girls told Jay it was nice meeting him and they hoped to see him around. They started walking ahead of England, so she could say goodbye.

"Well, Jay, I'm glad I met you."

"Not as glad as I am to have met you. I need to get your digits so we can keep in touch."

"Okay."

Jay and England exchanged numbers. Jay told England he'd call her one day next week. She said that would be fine and they went their separate ways. England walked fast to catch up with the girls. They had two more workshops and they'd be finished for the day. The next workshop was about dorm life and how to cope with issues related to your roommate.

As the college counselor discussed dormitory living, she stated that some girls stay up all night while others go to sleep. Some girls don't make curfew, and some do. Some girls even get sent home for having boys in the room. That was the part that got their attention. Now they knew—no boys in the dorm rooms, only in the lobby area. The counselor suggested that you and your roommate set some rules for both to follow. This should be done at the beginning. Once the rules were in place, no one could make excuses for not being respectful or thoughtful.

The final workshop was the health workshop. The nurse told them about various clinics that would be on campus and what type of situations they can handle. Some clinics could charge a small fee for the services, while others may include the fee in the tuition. She alluded to the fact that staying healthy and keeping fit were the keys to a great college experience. She also discussed diabetes and how to keep it under control.

She told the workshop participants that drug usage was heavy at some college campuses. They should be aware of the date-rape drugs that were out there. She showed the workshop participants some of the new drugs that were out there. She stated that if they went to a party, they should go with a group and make sure they didn't leave their drinks to go to the bathroom. They shouldn't trust people to watch their drinks while they stepped away. In fact, they shouldn't trust anyone to take care of them. They were their own responsibility, not their friends' responsibility.

Secondly, she talked about safe sex. She said the only way to be truly safe is to abstain from having sex. However, if you insisted on having sex, you would be putting yourself at risk for diseases. She told the group that most colleges have more girls than boys, and boys tend to have more sex partners than girls. She told them to always know their partner's status before having sex.

Next, she gave out information on STDs and HIV. England and Gabby already knew the statistics, but it was good to get a confirmation on their research. While the presenter was talking about this, a lot of people seemed on edge, and she noticed. She went straight to the pictures to show them what several STDs could do to a person's body.

The pictures made a dramatic statement. She pointed out that half of the newly infected HIV population was under the age of 25. She informed her audience that people who have HIV could look perfectly healthy. If they took care of themselves and took their medicine, no one would know they had the virus. She noted that HIV was a virus that had spread all over the world like wildfire. It had hit the college campuses hard. Why? Students were under a lot of peer pressure, lack of maturity, used alcohol and drugs, and there was a growing incidence of date rape. Not only that, but some students come to college already HIV positive.

In conclusion, she told them to make prevention a high priority. "If you're not having sex or using drugs, don't start. Those who are sexually active or using drugs," she said, "must seek counseling and go get tested. You are at risk," she pointed out, "and are not invincible. Her final words were, "I hope all of you have an exciting and safe year in college."

Chapter 18

England

I t was Monday morning and England had enjoyed a long weekend. On top of that, she didn't sleep much Saturday or Sunday night, so she was dead tired and not in the mood for foolishness. England entered the classroom.

"Good morning, England, you're late."

"I know. Here's my late slip."

"Okay people, pair up with your partner and complete last week's project, which is due on Wednesday."

The class started rearranging desks and chairs so they would have enough room to complete their projects. England's partner had already set up their station and beckoned for England to join her.

"England, girl, what's wrong with you?"

"Melissa, let's just finish our project."

Melissa frowned.

"Okay, I was just wondering, that's all."

"Right, we need to check our hypothesis before we go any further."

"Okay. It's on."

After first period, England started down the hall. Gabby had to walk fast to catch up with her. England was worried about Nikki. The information they received in the health workshop was more than they could handle. The STD pictures the nurse showed were really graphic and repugnant. Some teens walked out for one reason or another. Those who stayed received a lesson that they would never forget. It put fear or anger in some of them, but for others it probably didn't mean a thing.

"England, wait up."

England continued to walk.

"England, slow down!" Gabby called. "I understand your concerns. Nikki is going to be fine. She must choose for herself. You can't tell her what to do. She's her own person. She has to be mature enough to realize she needs to go get the test, so she can save herself. So, stop beating yourself up over this."

Gabby grabbed England by the arm and yanked her. England finally stopped.

"England, don't do this to yourself."

"You're right, Gabby."

England walked a little faster.

"Nikki has her own decisions to make in her life. But that doesn't mean that I'm not afraid for her."

The girls went to their next two classes very quietly. Ken noticed that they were distant. He wondered what was going on but was willing to wait until lunchtime to ask them. In the meantime, he was searching for clues and searching their faces for answers. He looked at England, then at Gabby. He did this about three times. He saw their sadness, anger, fear, and restlessness. He didn't see the confidence that they both usually showed. Now he was getting a little concerned. After class, Ken beat them to the door of the classroom so he wouldn't get left behind.

"Hey, what's up, ladies?"

"Nothing," said Gabby.

England didn't say a word.

"Well, Gabby, I guess you're speaking for England too."

England turned on her toes and looked Ken in the eye.

"Not today, Ken!" yelled England, before turning around and walking off.

Ken couldn't say a word. He just stopped in his tracks, looked to the floor, and then up again. By then the girls were out the door and going down the steps, leaving a trace of their silhouette behind them.

"England, did you have to be so mean?"

"He makes me sick."

"Why?"

"He's the one that got all of this started. If it were not for him sharing his daddy's sex books, Nikki and Calvin wouldn't be in the shape they're in."

"I'm angry too, knowing we may lose a friend anytime. But I will not blame Ken for this."

"Well, who do we blame? The companies that distribute the sex books? The grownups who purchase them? Or the kids who snoop around in their parents' personal things and find them?"

"I think they all play a part in this tragedy."

England was getting a little calmer. "You're right, Gabby. Nikki must decide if she wants to know whether she's HIV positive or negative. It has to be her choice, not mine. I will not pressure her anymore. I'm just scared for her. You heard those numbers the nurse was calling out. That is a bit much, don't you think?"

"Yes, England, I heard the numbers—850,000 to 950,000 Americans are living with HIV, and one in four are unaware of their infection."

England chimed in. "And Black women account for 72% of all the new HIV cases in women."

"To add to that," Gabby said, "67% of the black women with HIV contracted it from heterosexual sex."

"And these are the statistics."

"The end."

"Gabby, that's not funny."

"What! I just said 'the end'."

"Seems to me you were trying to get a laugh."

"No, England, the stats are real, and we're all fortunate to receive the information that was given to us this past weekend at the seminar. We know that there are a lot of HIV cases on college campuses. We just have to abide by the rules we've set for ourselves, regardless of what people may say about us. We must truly stay close to God. He is our strength and our source. What's for lunch?"

"I really don't have an appetite," said England.

"Well, you gotta eat something."

"I know. I guess I'll just have a salad."

"Okay," Gabby said. "Mickey D's, here we come."

"Why McDonald's?"

"They have the best fries."

The girls hurried off to the neighborhood McDonald's down the street from their high school. Gabby bobbed her head slightly to the music that was blasting from the car speakers. They pulled up to the drive-thru, waiting for someone to ask them for their order. After a couple minutes of waiting, a voice finally came through the intercom.

"Hello, sorry for the wait. May I take your order?"

"Hi, I would like a salad with grilled chicken and a Cheeseburger Happy Meal."

"Is the happy meal for a boy or girl?"

England and Gabby started laughing.

"It's for a girl."

"What type of drinks?"

"Cokes."

"Thank you. Drive to the first window, please."

"She forgot to tell us how much."

"I know, right?"

After the girls got their lunch, they headed back to campus. Instead of going to the cafeteria, they ate in the car while listening to the music. Marvin Gaye came on singing, "Let's Get It On," then a song by Lil Wayne. Other students were passing by dancing to the beat of the music. Since Lil Wayne was getting so much attention, England decided she would turn the volume up louder. It drew a crowd and kids were dancing all over the school lawn. They were making such a big commotion that the principal sent one of the school officers to check things out. By that time England and Gabby had gotten out of the car and were dancing with their classmates.

The school officer radioed in to tell the principal that things were okay. The seniors were just dancing during their lunch break. The principal told him to tell them to turn off the music and go to class. Lunch was over. Gabby turned the music off, locked her car doors, and walked to class. The students were not very happy with the fact that they had to end their block party.

"Boooo!" said one boy.

"Party pooper!" said another.

"Hey it's okay. It's almost time for us to get out of here. We reign!" said another student.

The students went back into the school, each going their separate ways. After school England decided she would ride the bus home instead of riding with Gabby. England lived close by, so she could easily walk to school, but she didn't care to. England arrived home and her mom was pruning the flower bushes.

"Hey, Mom! Why are you pruning the flower bushes this time of year?"

"Hi, England, how was your day?"

"Great, why are you cutting the bushes?"

"I'm tired of them looking all wild."

"You know you may not have flowers next spring."

"Yes, I know."

"Okay, have fun, mom."

"Mmmm."

England went to the kitchen to get a glass of water and a snack. She checked the pots to see if there was anything cooking. Then she dashed upstairs to her bedroom. She turned on the TV and the radio, and she changed the stations. Suddenly she stopped and looked at the TV, while turning down the sound on her stereo. She turned the volume up on the TV, listening to every word the news anchor was saying. The phone rang three times, yet England didn't answer. All of a sudden, she heard her voice on her answering machine, and then a male voice. She didn't recognize the voice until the caller said his name.

"Hello, England, I hope all is well. I told you I was going to call. This is Jay."

England scrambled to get to the phone.

"Hello! Hello!"

"Why are you yelling?"

"Because I was trying to get the phone."

"How are you?"

"I'm doing well. And yourself?"

"Just great, now that I'm talking to you."

"What's going on?"

"Nothin' much. I was thinking about you and decided to give you a shout out."

"Well, that's nice of you," said England. "I was just looking at the news."

"The news. I hate the news."

"Why?"

"It is so sad and negative," said Jay. "It has more drama than anything."

"It has some good qualities also."

"Like what?"

"Well, it keeps you informed about current events, it tells you about the stock market, it gives you the weather report, and gives you the drop load on politics..."

"Yeah, I guess you're right, but the local drama can cease."

"I hear you."

"So, England, are you dating anyone?"

"No, not right now. What about you?"

"I don't know. My girlfriend broke up with me a couple days ago."

"So, is that the reason for the call?"

"No, I had plans to call you anyway. Why would I allow that situation to affect my plans?"

"I just thought I'd ask."

"I would like to take you out. I know you're going to ask why, so I'm prepared to answer that question."

"No. I wasn't going to ask you that. I know I look good and have a great personality. Why wouldn't you want to take me out?"

"Gosh, you're so confident. Are you always like this?"

"Maybe."

"I guess I'll find out on my own," said Jay. "So do you want to go out Friday night?"

"Yeah, we can do that. Where would you like to go?"

"To the movies and then out for pizza."

"Okay, just let me know where to meet you."

"Where to meet me?"

"Yes. What did you expect?"

"I thought I would pick you up at your house," said Jay.

"Oh no, I don't know you like that. I need to get to know you better before we start riding together."

"Okay, but I am not a rapist nor a killer."

"I didn't say you were," replied England. "Just think—if you had a sister, would you want her to get in the car with someone she met for the first time?"

"You've been watching too many hostile shows. But I get your

127

point. You need to be safe and feel safe. I want you to feel safe with me, so I will play by your rules. You're the boss."

"I am not the boss. I just want to be careful."

"I understand. I'll call you on Thursday night to tell you the specifics."

"Okay."

"Bye, England, and have a great evening."

"Bye, and you do the same."

England hung up the phone and went downstairs to see if her mom had started dinner. When she got to the kitchen entrance, she didn't smell anything cooking. So, she went searching for her mother. England found her lounging on the sofa drinking a cold beverage. England stood over her mother looking down on her.

"Mom, what's for dinner?"

"Your dad is bringing supper home tonight."

"Well, I'm hungry. What time is he coming home?"

"Soon."

"Soon! What does that mean?"

"Just soon."

England picked up the phone and dialed her dad's cell phone. He answered on the second ring.

"Hello."

"Hey, Dad, when are you bringing dinner?"

"I'm pulling up as we speak."

England hung up the phone and ran to the door.

"Hey, England."

"Dad, what ya bring?"

"Fried fish, hushpuppies, and coleslaw."

"Yummy, I'm hungry."

"Okay, we better get something in your stomach before you start chomping on fingers."

England helped her dad carry the bags toward the kitchen while her dad headed to the entertainment room in search of Mom. After she finished eating, she joined her parents in the entertainment room.

"Hi Mom and Dad, whatcha doing?"

"Just talking, what's up with you?"

"I got a date for Friday."

"Whaaat, who is he?"

"His name is Jay Anderson."

"Okay, does he go to your school?"

"No."

"Well, where did you meet him?" inquired her dad.

"I met him at that seminar last weekend."

"Tell us more."

"There's not much to tell. He is a senior, he has several scholarships, he will be attending ASU, and he has a very high GPA."

"Who are his parents and what high school does he attend?"

"I don't know anything about his parents, and we did not discuss our schools."

England already knew what her dad was going to say.

"Well, that's not a problem. If he is such a great athlete, I should be able to pull up his stats. Then we can see what school he attends."

Mr. Desto started up his laptop and typed Jay's full name into the search box. Bama! His name and picture popped up.

"All right! Here we go. His stats are good. He is an All-American player. Wow! Honey! This boy is holding a 4.0 GPA! That is awesome, and he plays football. He not only plays football, but he also plays baseball, and he wrestles."

"And holding on to a 4.0 GPA?" said Mrs. Desto.

"Yeah!" said England. "And he's nice and very respectful."

"We'll be the judge of that," replied Mr. Desto.

"So will he be picking you up?" asked Mrs. Desto.

"No. I thought we could meet out for pizza and a movie."

"So, you just change our rule?" asked Mr. Desto.

"No, I just thought I would gather more information about him, then invite him over," said England.

"You thought, huh?"

"Daaaad! Why are you looking like that?"

"Here's the deal," Mr. Desto said. "He will come here Friday night for dinner and conversation. If we like him, he can take you out another time."

"Oh, my goodness, Dad! I'm on my way to college and you're still treating me like a kid. Mommmm! Aren't you going to say something?"

"I agree with your dad."

"We just want to make sure he understands where we're coming from."

"Oh, my goodness, Dad."

England walked off pouting. She went upstairs to her room to call Jay.

"Hello."

"Hi England. How are you?"

"Well, I guess I'm okay."

"You don't sound okay," Jay said. "What's wrong?"

"Well, my dad won't let me meet you to hang out tomorrow."

"Okay, but why not?"

"He said he needs to meet you first."

"And what's wrong with that?"

"Man, my dad is going to get you over here and ask a whole lot of personal questions. I don't want him to do that."

"So, you think I can't handle your dad?"

"I didn't say that. I just know he can be hardcore with his questions."

"You must have been dating some knuckleheads that don't know how to think when they're in the hot seat."

"You sound as if this would be fun."

"No, I think your dad needs to interview me. There's nothing wrong with that. He needs to know the character of your friends, that's all."

"I told him you were nice and respectful."

"I know he laughed at that," Jay said. "England, let me share something with you. Good fathers are always interested in who their daughters are dating. People are crazy these days and there are a lot of loose teenagers. Your father was a boy before he became a man. He dated and had ideas of what he was going to do on a date. He probably was wild or had to listen to wild stories from his friends about girls."

"You think so?"

"He's only looking out for your interests, and I don't blame him at all. I have a younger sister and I have to look out for her as well."

"I didn't know you had a sister."

"Yes, and she is a handful."

"What grade?"

"She's in the ninth and thinks she knows everything about boys, when she has no clue at all."

"Is she dating?"

"Trying to, but she knows she can't right now."

"So, what is it that you want to do on Friday?"

"I'm coming to your house to meet your folks, unless you don't want to go out with me."

"I do want to go out with you."

"Well, we will just do what your dad wants us to do. I'll see you at six on Friday."

"Okay, see you then."

"Bye."

England hung up the phone. She thought Jay had no clue of what he was getting himself into. She smiled and thought he was going to get murdered. No one had been able to pass Mr. Desto's test. He always had her male friends sweating bullets. After they left, he would laugh so hard that he started crying. However, he never told England who to hang out with or date. He would just point out some key factors about her friends. He really gave her something to think about, and she always made her decision with the help of his information.

Mr. Desto used this tactic for several reasons. One, he wanted England to know that he was a part of her life. Kids whose parents are not a part of their lives and don't know their friends usually end up in trouble. Two, she has to be careful who she allows to enter her life. Some people have negative motives for entering your life. Three, she needed to make sure she got enough information on the person and his family. Lack of information may cause problems later on down the road. We all have to be careful about the company we keep. The company we keep could influence our behavior and attitude.

Friday came and England watched the clock in school all day. In her mind she kept visiting her closet, trying to figure out what outfit and shoes she was going to wear. As England stared into space, Gabby tried to get her attention.

"England. England!"

"What!" England interrupted class with her yelling.

"Ms. Desto, do you have a problem?"

"No, ma'am."

"Girl, what's wrong with you?" England said. "Trying to get me in trouble?"

"No," Gabby replied, "I just wanted to make sure you got the changes Mrs. Barlow just made."

"What note? What change?"

"Girl, what's wrong with you? You been off base all day, watching the clock and everything."

The bell rang and the girls left the class.

They were walking down the hallway to get books out of their lockers when Ken approached them.

"Hey, you two."

"Hey, Ken," the girls said in unison.

"What's up for the night?"

"Well, my ballet company is performing in Macon," Gabby said, "so I got to go home and get ready for that."

"And you, England, do you want to hang out?"

"No, I have already made plans."

"You have?" Gabby said.

"Yes, Gabby, I have plans tonight."

Gabby looked surprised, trying to figure out what England was talking about, but she dared not ask the question in front of Ken.

"I guess I'm just like Gabby," said Ken. "Who are you going out with? Nikki?"

"No, I haven't talked to Nikki since last weekend," England replied.

"She still has not called?"

"No."

"Where were you all last weekend?" Ken asked.

After closing the lockers, they walked out towards the students' parking lot.

"We went downtown to College Day," said Gabby.

"How was that?"

"It was great," said England. "You should have been there."

"But who are you going out with?"

"I am going out with a friend," said England.

"Boy or girl?"

"Why?"

"Nothing, I just thought I'd ask."

"Ken, how are your mom and dad?"

"Oh, they are great, Gabby. Thanks for asking."

132

"Well, have you seen Calvin lately?"

"Yes."

"How is he?"

Ken shook his head. "He's not looking good at all."

"How is his mom?"

"She's doing the best she can."

"Well, has he been able to call any of those girls he slept with?" asked England.

"We've been trying to contact as many as possible."

"What do you mean by 'we'?"

"I've been doing most of the calling for him."

"Boy, I am so sorry that you have to do that," said Gabby.

"Me, too!" said England.

"That has to be the worst experience you have had to encounter."

"Yes, it has been a little too much."

"Well, don't do it anymore, Ken," said England. "Just don't do it."

"I have to, England. Who else is going to do it? I can't ask his mother to do it. That will bring her even more pain."

"Ken, you are a great friend to Calvin."

"Well, I gotta go. I will talk to you ladies later."

"Bye."

"Bye, Ken," said England.

"Man, I thank you, Jesus," said Gabby. "I am glad that I'm not in his shoes or in the shoes of the girls he's calling."

"We are at the age where we're just supposed to enjoy life."

"With parental guidance."

"Some kids get into trouble when they *have* parents guiding them," England pointed out.

"Those kids are just hard-headed. They can't see their future."

"At this age we are not all that innocent, huh?"

"I think this is a learning stage for us," said Gabby. "We're supposed to be learning how to cope with issues. But some of us get in our own way and make life miserable."

"Like Calvin and Ken, huh?"

"Yep, Calvin and Ken are prime examples, but I don't think they had much guidance."

"Ken did," said England. "Our preacher talked to him."

133

"But was he listening? Or did he tune the preacher out?"

"Now *that* I can't answer for you."

"Okay, then answer this," Gabby said. "Who are you going out with?"

"You remember Jay?"

"Talking about the guy you met last weekend, the football player?"

"Yes."

"Did your dad meet him already?" Gabby asked.

"No."

"Well, how are you going out with him?"

"I'm not," said England. "He's coming over tonight for dinner."

"Oh, I was getting ready to say old pops is slacking."

"No, he made it very clear that he needs to take him through his silly test."

"That's going to be funny," chuckled Gabby. "Do you think he'll pass?"

"Girl, he told me he's not afraid of my dad and will pass his test."

"Oh no! He is bold. I want to be there!"

"Sorry, no spectators."

The girls got in their separate cars, promising to call each other on Saturday. England pulled out of the parking lot, still trying to decide what to wear for dinner. By the time she reached the driveway of her house, she had decided to let her mom pick out her outfit. As soon as she parked, she ran into the house calling her mom.

"Mom! Mom! Mom!"

England's mom was not home. She ran to the kitchen to see if her mom had put a note on the board. She hadn't. England called her mom on her cell phone. Her mom didn't answer, so she left a message. She went upstairs and started going through her closet, pulling out clothes she might want to wear. While she was upstairs, her mom came in through the door that led to the garage.

"England!"

England didn't answer, so her mom called her cell phone.

"Mom, I'm on my way down."

England went downstairs and to the kitchen.

"Hi, Mom."

"Hey, England, how was your day?"

"Fine, and yours?"

"Great. TGIF!"

"I don't know what to wear tonight, so I need your help."

"You need my help?"

"Yes."

England's mom turned around and looked at her.

"Wow! You must like him. You have always put together a sharp outfit."

"I know, right? Why can't I just put on something without thinking about it?"

"If you are actually thinking about it, that means you like him."

"Okay, are you going to help me?"

"Yes, but we are having seafood."

"So, I need something that will complement the dinner?"

"Yes, like jeans and a nice top."

"That's it?"

"Yes."

England ran upstairs. She called Jay to confirm and tell him what was for dinner. She went back through her closet one more time, looking for a soft blouse to wear with her jeans. After that, she took her shower and headed back downstairs with the video camera and stand. While setting up the stand in the dining room, Mr. Desto walked in.

"England, what are you doing?"

"I am setting up my camera so I can capture every moment."

"What do you mean?"

"Well, Dad, you said this was an interview, and I don't want to miss anything just in case I need to go to the bathroom or something."

"I really don't think you need to video this. It's just a get-acquainted dinner."

"Yeah, with Mr. Desto as the starring actor," said England.

"What will Jay think?" Mr. Desto asked.

"Oh, he'll like it. He's used to interviews. It won't scare him."

"So, I won't scare him? Is that what you're trying to say?"

"No Dad, he's just used to being out front, that's all."

"Mmmm."

Mr. Desto walked away. England adjusted the lens of the camera. Inwardly she was dying laughing. She was hoping that her dad would back down once he knew he was going to be taped, but he didn't. He still had time to change his mind. Maybe he wouldn't be so hard on

Jay with the camera rolling, thought England. England's mom came into the kitchen with her apron on, ready to cook.

"England, what are you doing?"

"Mom, I am setting up my camera so I can tape the interview."

"You've got to be kidding me."

"No, I'm not."

"Is this necessary?"

"Yes, I don't want to miss anything."

"Your dad is going to trip when he sees this."

"He saw it."

"What did he say?"

"The same thing you said. But I don't think he is going to go all the way. What do you think?"

"Ooooh! I get it. You think your dad is going be softer with Jay because he's on camera?"

"Don't you?"

"No. He's just going to be more tenacious."

"What will scare dad off? I can't have him asking a million questions. Maybe we should set a limit to the number of questions he can ask."

"There is no limit. Don't worry, your dad is not going to embarrass you. As a matter of fact, you need to make sure you ask all the questions you need to ask, too."

"I think Dad will leave no stone unturned."

The doorbell rang and England rushed to the door. She was trying to make sure that she beat her dad there. Her mom came out of the kitchen and her dad came out of the entertainment room. They met halfway down the foyer. England opened the door and greeted Jay. He had two bunches of flowers in his hands. He greeted England and gave her the first bunch.

"Jay, these are nice. You didn't have to do this."

"Yes, I did. I have to bring flowers to the lady of the house and her daughter I'm going to take out—if I pass her dad's interview."

"Come, let's go meet my parents."

England and Jay walked through the foyer.

"Mom! Dad!"

"We're right here."

"Mom, Dad, this is Jay. Jay, these are my parents, Mr. and Mrs. Desto."

"Hi, Jay, nice to meet you."

"Nice to meet you, Jay."

Mr. Desto extended his hand.

"Well, it's nice to meet both of you. Mrs. Desto the flowers are for you."

"Thank you, Jay, I like flowers."

Mr. Desto looked surprised.

"Well, let's go have a seat in the sitting area."

England walked fast to get her camera and stand. When she returned, they were already in conversation. Her mom was sitting close to her dad, as he started with his first set of questions.

"So, Jay, England tells me that she met you last Saturday at the college fair."

"Yes, that's true."

"So, did you enjoy the fair?"

"Yes, I did, although I already know where I'm going to college, I wanted to check out some of the seminars to see if I could be further enlightened by the workshops that were being offered."

"Well, were you?" asked Mrs. Desto.

"Yes. I enjoyed the health workshop, and the one about being safe on the yard. I mean campus."

"Hey, that's okay. We've heard that term before."

"England tells us that you will be attending ASU on a football and academic scholarship, and that you play three different sports and still maintain a high GPA."

"Yes sir, that's correct. I have a 4.0 average. I play football, baseball, and I'm a wrestler."

England was trying to focus the camera and her dad was a little bit distracted by the taping. He glanced at the camera and then looked away. England noticed his uneasiness through the lens. However, her dad kept pushing the questions.

"Tell me, how did you manage to do all of that as a high school boy?"

"Well, I have a mentor who has been in my life since I was about ten. He has done an awesome job with me, as far as preparing me and teaching me about how to make positive decisions in my life. He set the rules and I followed the game plan. He had me create a schedule for myself and he made me stick to it. I'm grateful for that and thank

God for blessing me with someone who could help me reach my fullest potential."

"I'm impressed," said Mrs. Desto.

"So am I. Now, tell me a little about your family."

England took a seat and let the camera roll.

"Okay. I live with my mother and sister, who's in the ninth grade. My mom was once a nurse at the hospital, but she quit because her hours were too long, and she didn't want us home by ourselves. Now she works at a doctor's office. My grandparents live in Philly, and we visit them every summer."

"Do you have a career choice or are your eyes set on the NFL?"

"Although I like football and baseball, my major will be political science and I would like to be a corporate lawyer. I have always wanted to be in law. I hope to attend a prestigious law school. I just don't know which one."

"Do you attend church?"

"Yes, I attend church every Sunday and I am on the junior usher board."

"What is your relationship with God?"

"I believe that God is my Savior. He is the head of my life. If it were not for Him placing people into my life, I would probably be a gangbanger or selling drugs, or robbing people. I know the odds are against young black men. I know that I have to stay on my p's and q's, because there are no equal rights for me. We, as black men, have to work smarter and sometimes harder to make it in this world. Look at me—I come from a single parent household. According to statistics, I am not supposed to have made it this far. But if it were not for God on my side I wouldn't have. So, you see, Mr. Desto, I figure if I live my life the way I'm supposed to, God will see to it that I make it and become successful."

"If you could go back and do something different in your life," Mr. Desto asked, "what would it be?"

"That's a tough question for me. I really don't know. I can't say I would go get my dad and put him in my life, because that may not be a good idea. I mean, I don't know him, and I don't know how he's living his life. However, I would like to meet him. I don't think I would make any changes. We have had our ups and downs just like any other family. I think I have had a very good life, considering I come from a single parent household. I have the greatest mentor ever. He has truly been a father figure for me. What I have learned from him has truly made my personality shine. I don't know what else to say."

Mrs. Desto excused herself to go cook the fish. She appeared to be very pleased with Jay's honesty. She felt that she could trust him with her daughter. England had a grin on her face, and she was feeling better now that she could sense her dad's comfort level growing. She knew that this interview was close to ending. This would be the first time that her dad stopped an interview early.

"Well, Jay, I appreciate your honesty. I must say that your mentor has truly done a great job with you. You are blessed to have such a man in your life."

"Thank you, Mr. Desto. I try my best to hold myself accountable for my actions and live by the rules that were set for me."

Mrs. Desto broke in from the kitchen.

"Okay, dinner is ready. Let's go eat."

"Jay, I hope you like fish."

"Yes ma'am. I love it!"

The Destos and Jay sat down for dinner. Mr. Desto blessed the food, and they all started passing the platters around the table.

Chapter 19

England and Gabby

It was 7:00 Monday morning. England and Gabby met up with each other by the media center.

"Good morning, England."

"Good morning. What took you so long?"

"I'm not late," said Gabby.

"No. But you normally would be waiting for me."

"That's correct. Why are you on time?"

"I got up early," replied England.

"Well, we should be on time for Christian meeting."

"Yes, we will."

"According to our conversation on Saturday," said Gabby, "Mr. and Mrs. Desto like Jay, huh?"

"Yeah, he is a joy to be around."

"So, when are you going to see him again?"

"Well, my dad says it's okay for us to go out this weekend," England replied. "But he has a tournament on Saturday."

"So, what's wrong with Friday night?"

"He doesn't go out the night before he performs. He said he needs all of his rest."

"Really! And you believe that?"

"It doesn't matter what I believe," said England. "It's what he says."

"Well, what are your thoughts on that?"

"I don't have any."

"Oh, really now!"

"Yes, Gabby."

"He is the most sought after young man I know," said Gabby. "You think he's playing it straight with you?"

"He has no reason to lie. I am not his girlfriend."

"But you would like to be."

"And!"

"Okay, I'll leave it alone."

England and Gabby entered the doorway of the gym, where a lot of kids had already created a circle. The coach, Mr. Jones, opened the meeting with prayer requests. Students took turns calling out friends and family members who were in need of prayer. Gabby called out Calvin's name. The students looked up at her and then Mr. Jones. England also looked at her with one eye open. After prayer, Mr. Jones told the students to get into their groups and read Romans 12:9-21 and answer the question, "What can you do this week, in a practical way, to 'live at peace' with someone who irritates you?" He reminded them to put their answers on the whiteboard, so others could comment.

"Okay, England, let's go get into our group."

"Hi, Gabby," said Michelle, after looking around for other members in the group.

"Hi, Michelle, how are you?"

"I'm good. What about you?"

"I'm just great. Where is the rest of our group?"

"Here they come. Let's go to the top of the bleachers."

"Okay."

The group of girls and boys walked up the bleachers and took seats.

"Let's take turn reading a verse," stated Michelle.

"I think we should read it quietly to ourselves first."

"That's good. We can do that."

Each person started reading Romans 12:9-21. As England read, she was jotting down notes. She looked at the question that Mr. Jones had assigned. She thought about China who she really did not care for. She thought of how China and her friends were very vindictive and spiteful. She thought about homecoming night, how she and her friends tried jumping on Nikki. She thought about how the crowd just went wild and how everybody started fighting. No, England did not like China at all. How could she be pleasant to her? The Bible says, "Love your enemy." How could she possibly do that? Where could she start?

Gabby was thinking the same thing. China had always been their enemy, ever since middle school. It was a conflict that had never been resolved. How could she resolve their differences? How could she give in to China? The Bible says, "Bless those who persecute you." Gabby shook her head from side to side; knowing that this was going to be a hard task for England and herself, but it must be done. The bell rang in the middle of everyone's thoughts. Students started getting up and putting on their backpacks. It was time for first period.

"You all don't forget to go to the website," shouted Mr. Jones, "to post your comments and respond to the posting of others."

"Okay, let's go to class."

"So, England, what are you going to post?"

"I don't know. I just know we were probably thinking about this one person who has been a part of our lives since middle school, and how she keeps on coming with a lot of smack. I'm getting tired of her and her smack."

"I know exactly who you're referring to," replied Gabby. "But how can we connect with her? She's our enemy. We know this, she knows this. As a matter of fact, everybody knows this."

"Well, I think we need to research our situation," said England. "Read all of Romans and search our hearts. Then, just maybe, we can come up with some alternative method to deal with her."

"That's a good point. I'll finish reading Romans tonight. Write down some points and then we can share later."

"That's a wrap."

Gabby and England went through their day lost in thought with little conversation. Every now and then one would make a gesture or say something. But for most of it they were distant. They decided they'd eat a salad in the cafeteria instead of going off campus for lunch. After getting their salads, they sat at their regular table and were beginning to eat when China and her friends came over. Gabby turned around to find China was standing over Gabby's left shoulder.

"Wow! I didn't know you were behind me."

"Didn't mean to frighten you," China said. "I wanted to know if we could sit with you and England."

Gabby looked at England, who nodded her head yes.

"Sure."

China and three of her friends sat down, while the other students looked on.

"It's been a while since you all have eaten in the café," said China.

"Yes, we've been in need of a lot of fresh air," replied Gabby.

"I see."

"Have you all heard or seen Calvin lately?"

"Yes, we've seen Calvin," said Gabby.

All of the girls looked up at Gabby, waiting for her to tell more.

"Well, how is he?" asked China. "He doesn't return my calls. It's just like he fell off the earth."

"He's doing well," said England. "He just decided to be home schooled since that last incident. You know the one at homecoming."

"Oh yeah," replied China, "he decided to stay home because he knows when I see him, he is going to wear a butt whippin'."

"Don't you mean 'whipping'?"

"Whateva!"

England just nodded her head.

"How come he talks to you and Gabby," said Monique, "but he won't talk to China?"

"Gabby and I are not the problem, China is."

"I am not his problem anymore," China said. "Once he tried to cheat on me I was done with him."

"How could you be done with someone," said Erica, "when you were the one cheating on him?"

"Boys always cheat. No matter what they tell you. You have to cheat on them first before they cheat on you, so when they do, you won't feel bad."

"Girl, you are wild," said Erica.

"She got it from her mama," said Monique.

England and Gabby were thinking the same thing. Since China had just admitted that she had slept with someone else besides Calvin, it was possible that she gave Calvin HIV. However, China had not been sick, nor had she missed any days out of school. England decided to ask a question to pull more information out of China. She figured if China didn't answer it, her friends were dying to answer it.

"So, China, you're the big star in school," England said. "You have more boyfriends than any guy has girlfriends. I guess you've beaten them at their game."

"Girl, never give all of yourself to a boy. They are so dumb and think they know the game. But my momma said we can play the game better."

"What are you talking about?"

"Don't just have one boyfriend, girl," said China.

"So, are you saying that you're sleeping with more than one guy?" asked England.

"China has them eating out the palm of her hands."

"You're not afraid of sexually transmitted diseases?"

"Girl, please," China said. "I have been having sex since I was about twelve."

"You think that's funny?" England said.

"No, I just grew up early. And I probably could teach you a thing or two."

China's friends started giggling.

This was an opportunity for England and Gabby to share what they had learned about teen sex.

"You can teach me a thing or two, huh?"

"Yes, I am experienced enough to teach."

"Have you taught all of them some of your tricks?"

"No, she isn't talking about me," said Erica. "I'm not having sex with nobody. My dad will beat my behind if I even think about it."

"But you have thought about it," said China.

"Yes, but never acted upon."

"Good for you," said Gabby."

"And the rest of you are having sex, huh?" asked England.

The girls nodded yes, except one.

"Sex is nothing, everybody's doing it," said China.

Some of the girls laughed.

"You all think this is funny?" asked England. "Don't you know how many teenagers have HIV right here in our school? Do you know how many are HIV positive here in our city? Do you know the statistics? As a matter of fact, do you know your status?"

Everyone at the table got quiet while England and Gabby started a serious dialogue about the subject. China and her friends were looking at Gabby and England as if they were from another planet, talking a language that they'd never heard. They were listening with ears opened. This information could help them if they cared to use it.

"I'm sorry to burst your bubble," blurted England. "I know you're popular for what you do and what you portray. But having sex is no laughing matter."

"There are kids our age being diagnosed every day with HIV," injected Gabby. "Do you know how they got it?"

Some of the girls shook their heads no, while at the same time giving Gabby the go ahead to tell more. Gabby continued to talk. She quoted doctors, speakers, and her parents. Gabby told them that there was an HIV epidemic among teenagers. Teenagers who take chances were falling victims of STDs and HIV. Most teenagers who suffered from an STD, the girls said, were unaware that they had one. Then they pass it to a sexual partner, and that partner passes it on to the next partner.

"Many STDs have no symptoms, and they can do great damage to the reproductive system if not treated in time."

"If you're sexually active, you're in danger of contracting an STD or even, AIDS," said England. "Do you know there are almost 900,000 people who have HIV?"

"No!" said the girls in unison.

"Y'all don't know what you're talking about," said China. "You been reading too much."

"Yeah, and you haven't been reading at all," replied England.

"HIV in Black women is on the rise," said Gabby. "We count for most of the cases that have been contracted lately."

"The number is very high when it comes to black teenagers," England continued. "It appears that teenagers take chances and refuse to listen to their parents, who are telling them that sex is not for kids or teenagers. Parents tell us to hold off on sex because we don't know all that we need to know. Besides, it's a grown-up thing, not meant for children."

"Well, my dad said you're supposed to be married when you become sexually active," said Erica."

"Your father is correct," said Gabby.

"That's a bunch of bull," said China. "You can have sex when you think you're ready."

"Not really," said Monique.

"Why do you think a lot of teens are infected with HIV?" asked Gabby. "They thought they were ready, and some thought they were invincible—they thought HIV couldn't touch them."

"They were wrong, "England added. "Years down the road they found out they were HIV positive. They had no symptoms for a long time. They were going about their business not thinking at all, just enjoying sex with many different partners. Then one day...."

"I suggest if you're sexually active" Gabby said, "go get tested for STDs and HIV. You might just save your life."

The bell rang and it was time to go to class. China put her tray away while the other girls huddled together, saying that they were going to pull the information up on the internet. England and Gabby hoped that they had gotten their point across. They knew that people had to make their own choices. But if they could give them enough information, it might help some of them make a positive, healthy choice.

"What do you think about what China said?" asked Gabby.

"China has low self-esteem. Her mother is probably the cause of it."

"You should be telling your daughter to keep herself, not beat the guys at their games, don't you think?"

"She thinks it's a game," said England. "I wonder if she gave Calvin HIV."

"No, I doubt it. I think Calvin had it before he hooked up with her."

"She has to be emotionally confused."

"Confused she is," said Gabby.

England and Gabby entered the class. Students were already preparing to take notes from the whiteboard. They sat down, pulled out their tablets, and started jotting notes. In the middle of their note taking, China sent England a message on a small sheet of paper. The note requested a meeting after school if they had time. England passed the note to Gabby. Gabby read it and nodded her head in agreement. Gabby was wondering what China wanted to talk about. She hoped they could call a truce, leave high school with no enemies, and go their separate ways.

After class, Ken waited for the girls.

"Hey, how's it going?"

"Hi, Ken. We're fine, just fine."

"What's going on Ken?"

"Nothin. How was your date last week?"

"It was great."

"Really? What's his name?"

"If you have to know, his name is Jay. No, he does not attend this school."

"Oh, I know that. He plays ball, he's in the band, what?"

"He plays ball."

"A jockey! Well, you are not his only girl."

"I didn't ask you," England replied. "And by the way, we're just friends."

"What is *he* saying? I'll bet if I asked him, he would tell me his version."

"Version! Boy, please. Nobody has a version. It's just what it is—friends!"

"Gabby," Ken said, "I know you don't believe England, do you?"

"What are you talking about?"

"I'm talking about Jay?"

"What about him?" asked Gabby. "Why are you in her business? I can't remember a time she was in yours."

"Okay, so it's like that."

"Come on, Gabby, let's go. Let's not continue to entertain his thoughts."

"Bye, Ken," said the girls in unison.

The girls walked to their next class, while Ken followed closely behind them. After completing all of their classes, they waited on the steps for China. England spotted China walking down the sidewalk alone. England and Gabby walked down the steps towards China. As they approached her, they saw such an awkward look on her face. They stood under the oak tree waiting for China to approach them.

As they waited, Ken came out the front door. As he glanced toward them, he saw China. It appeared to him that she was going to join them under the oak tree. Ken could not believe his eyes. All sorts of thoughts were racing through his mind. He was wondering if they were going to tell her the truth about Calvin. Then he thought maybe they were going to just work through their differences. The girls looked very calm, so he knew that they weren't angry. China looked very unsure of herself. She almost looked needy. But he let that thought go in a hurry. He had never known China to need anybody. She had always been able to handle her own problems. However, she did look different. This was not the China he had seen in the halls of the school, in the cafeteria, or at sporting events. Ken observed their surroundings, looking to see if China's friends were going to jump from behind cars or run from behind the building to ambush the pair. Instead of getting in his car, he decided to call England on her cell phone.

"Hi."

"Hi, I see you guys under the tree," Ken said. "I was making sure everything was okay before I leave."

"Yes, we're fine. Everything's cool."

"Okay, call me if you need me."

"Okay, thanks."

England and Ken hung up the phone. Ken got in his car and left.

"So, what's up?" England said to China.

"I was thinking. You said that you all have seen Calvin, right?" China said.

"Yes."

"Well, how can I see him?"

"Have you tried going by his house?" Gabby asked.

"No," China said.

"Does his mom know you?"

"Yes, I've been there several times."

"Have you tried talking to his mom?"

"No."

"Well, try his home line and talk with his mom," England said.

"I know there's more going on than what you all have told me," China said. "I just tried to play it off by saying what I said. You know—about kicking his butt."

"Yeah, I remember," said England.

"The only thing I can suggest is to talk with his mom." said Gabby.

"Ken won't even talk with me anymore."

"Well, don't worry about Ken," England suggested. "Just try to talk to Calvin or his mom. You might have to pay them a visit."

"Yes, I agree, just try to talk to Calvin," Gabby said. "But in the meantime, while you're trying to decide the best way to do that, you should go get tested for STDs."

"Why do you think I need one of those?" asked China.

"You have put yourself at risk of contracting an STD or HIV."

"You need to know your status and take care of yourself," added Gabby. "No one will take care of you, but you."

"Those guys you slept with are not thinking about you at all," said England. "As a matter of fact, they have moved on to the next victim."

"Y'all talk about it like it's not natural, like it's dangerous," said China.

"Sex is natural," said England. "We are animals, human animals. Having sex is a part of life. However, it can mess with your mind or, should I say, it can put you in a chaotic state. It can affect you emotionally and mentally, if you don't know how to handle all that comes with having sex."

"We went to a college forum a couple weeks ago," Gabby added. "They had a lot of workshops that helped us prepare for college. I still have those pamphlets. If you'd like, I can bring them to you. I'm sure you can gain some knowledge by reading this stuff."

"Sure, I'd like for you to bring them."

"Is there anything else you would like to talk about?"

"Well, I owe both of you a big apology," China said. "I am so sorry for acting nasty toward you. I was jealous because you all seem so together, not worrying about anything—just enjoying yourself, making good grades, and knowing your limits."

"China, you have to be true to yourself," Gabby replied. "You have to love you, take care of you, respect you, and know what you want out of life."

"Most of all, you have to have a relationship with God." England took out her Bible.

China's eyes got big. "You bring the Bible to school!"

"We are members of a Christian organization," said England, "so we have to bring our Bibles."

Gabby said, "Check out the front of it— 'God's Game Plan.' "

"It's designed with students in mind. It has a lot of real-life questions in here. It also gives us situations to elaborate on. It's really good."

China took the Bible and looked through it.

"Wow! So, this is what you rely on?"

"Yes, it's brought us this far. Coach Jones will let you come to the

BARBARA MURRELL, ED. D.

meetings. You don't have to be an athlete. If you want to make changes in your life, come to the meeting or talk with Coach Jones."

"I'll think about it." China gave England back her Bible.

"Well, I guess we'll go now," Gabby said. "Do you need a ride home?"

"No, I live nearby. I think I'll walk home and get some fresh air. This is a nice day to walk."

"Okay. See you later," China.

"Bye."

The girls walked to the car, hoping they had planted a seed in China's life. They hoped China would seek some help and gain some knowledge.

Chapter 20

England and Gabby

The prom was right around the corner, and England would be going to two proms. She was so excited, but her dad's wallet was not. England told her dad that she would need two dresses. He didn't understand why she couldn't wear the one dress twice. He was thinking that since the proms would be in two different counties, it didn't make sense to buy two dresses. On the other hand, Mrs. Desto agreed with England and believed that two dresses were indeed necessary.

"England, you and your mom have this idea that it's going to take two dresses to go to these proms. I disagree, because you're going to be in different counties, and no one will know you at his prom."

"Yes, they will. Some of the kids at church will be at both proms. That's why I need two dresses."

"I wear the same suit sometimes two days in the same week," Mr. Desto protested. "No one notices."

"Yes, they do," England replied. "But that's okay. You're a man. Normal people don't look at your clothing like they look at a female's attire."

"I bet Jay is going to wear that same tux."

"Maybe, but no one will notice because most tuxedos look alike anyway."

"Okay. I'm done. I'm not getting anywhere."

"Good."

England ran upstairs and jumped on the phone to call Gabby. England was anxious to speak to her, but Gabby didn't pick up. England hung up the phone and called Jay. To her surprise, he answered.

"Hello."

"Hello, Jay. How are you?"

"I'm doing well, and yourself?"

"I'm doing much better," England said, "since my dad agreed to purchase two dresses for the proms."

"Why do you need two?"

"Two proms, two different dresses."

"No one knows you at my school."

"That's what my dad said. But he forgot that people who attend our church live all over Atlanta. As a matter of fact, I know some kids at your school."

"Who? How come you never told me?"

"It wasn't a big deal."

"Until I asked you to the prom, huh?"

"Yep."

"Well, I can't wait to have your gorgeous self under my arm."

"May I ask you a question?"

"Sure, shoot!"

"You are in the spotlight at your school. I know that any girl would have loved to go to the prom with you. Why didn't you ask one of those young ladies to the prom?"

"You are correct," Jay replied. "I could have asked any random girl and she would have said yes. However, I chose not to ask them because I've been around my classmates for four years, and I've heard a lot of negative things about the girls at my school. I know a lot of stuff about my fellow teammates that isn't pretty. I asked you because I'm almost sure I will see something totally different in you than I have seen in all of my other dates. You have such zeal. You are full of confidence and know what you want. The girls I know at my school have too much game. I don't have time for it. They have guys fighting over them and acting just like jerks. I don't get down like that. And another thing, they are so sexual. It's just wild! I can't even describe the way they act and I'm not even sure I want to."

"I guess craziness is everywhere," England said. "My high school is a trip, too."

"So, are you excited about going to the prom with me?"

"Yes, I am. But I'm excited about everything. The school year will end soon and we'll be starting college. I'm nervous about that."

"Yeah, I hear you. You'll do well. You'll probably come home every weekend until you get used to it."

"No, I will be cheering."

"Oh, yeah? You and Gabby will be traveling with the football team. That's good; I can keep my eye on you."

England got another call. She looked at the number and noticed that it was Gabby.

"Hey, that's Gabby returning my call. I'll talk to you later, okay?"

"Okay, tell Gabby I said hello."

"Bye."

England clicked over.

"Hi."

"Hi, girl, you called?"

"Yeah, I was calling to tell you that my dad agreed to purchase both dresses."

"Good. I'm glad to hear that. He doesn't know you had already ordered both before you asked him."

"I just assumed he was going to say yes. I'm glad that mom told him I needed two dresses. You know he is not going to say no to her."

"No, he has to keep wifey happy."

"Okay, we'll talk later."

"Okay, bye."

Several weeks went by and it was time for England and Gabby to go to the prom. England was going to Jay's prom while Gabby was going to Matthew's. This was the night they'd all waited for.

Gabby was just as nervous as England. They were going to proms where they thought they wouldn't know anyone. Gabby was hoping that the people were friendly at Matthew's prom. England confided in Gabby that Jay said he could have asked any girl at his school to the prom, and she would have said yes, but he wanted to take England instead. England was sure she would get some rolling of the eyes, but she wasn't so concerned about that. She was just nervous because of her date with Jay. She and Gabby were talking on speakerphone while getting dressed, sharing their thoughts and concerns. Since they were going to two separate proms, they decided to eat dinner together. Their meeting place was Paul and Pino's. Matthew had made the reservation for four. The couples would meet up at 5:30.

England was dressed in a gorgeous fuchsia silk gown, while Gabby was inspired by the color purple. The girls looked very savvy and picturesque. Their parents were breathless. Their mothers' eyes were full of tears and their dads' hearts were pumping blood at a steady rate while they looked at their daughters with protective love and care. They were sure they'd done a great job in raising their daughters. They expected the young men to be on their best behavior, showing respect at all times. They hoped that the kids would enjoy the night and have a memory to cherish.

The doorbell rang at England's house. Her dad answered the door.

"Hi, Jay, come on in."

"Hi Mr. Desto. How are you this evening?"

"I'm doing well. Don't you look good!"

"Thank you, Mr. Desto."

"Well, I have my camera in the other room."

"I invited my mom, my mentor and my sister over. I hope you don't mind."

"Oh no, I'm glad you did."

"I just didn't want to waste time going back home to take pictures," Jay said, "so I invited my family to come here."

"Well, that was a smart idea."

The doorbell rang again. Mr. Desto answered it.

"Hi, I am Mr. Desto, England's father."

"I am Ms. Andrews, this is my daughter Lily, and this is Jay's mentor, Mr. Bradley. I hope you and your wife don't mind us coming over unannounced."

"No, that's fine."

"It's nice to meet you, Mr. Desto," said Ms. Andrews. "Jay told me about your interview with him. I thought that was interesting."

"Yes, I hope he said good things about it."

"Oh, he did. He was impressed."

"Well, come on in. England should be on her way down the stairs."

Mr. Desto didn't have any time alone with Jay. He wanted to make sure Jay was going to dinner and straight to the prom. After the prom, he wanted to make sure Jay was going to bring England straight home. But Mr. Desto didn't need to worry. Mr. Bradley, Jay's mentor had trained Jay to be nothing but a gentleman. This was the night that Jay would put all his training to use.

England was on her way downstairs and her mother was behind her.

"Oh, boy! Girl, you look good!" Mr. Desto started snapping pictures.

"I totally agree," said Jay.

England was blushing.

Jay met England by the stairs to help her down the last step. Mr. Desto was still snapping pictures. Mrs. Desto came from behind him, smiling. Mr. Desto stopped taking pictures long enough to introduce her to Jay's mother, sister, and mentor.

"Honey, this is Jay's mom, Ms. Andrews, his sister Lily, and mentor, Mr. Bradley."

"Hi, and welcome to our home."

"It's nice meeting you, Mrs. Desto, and thanks for having us."

"Not a problem."

"You have a beautiful daughter."

"Thanks."

England and Jay headed their way so that Jay could introduce his family to her.

"Mom, this is England. England this is my mom, Ms. Andrews."

"Nice meeting you, England. You are so pretty."

"Thanks."

"This is my sister, Lily."

"Hi, Lily."

"Hi, England."

"This is my mentor, Mr. Bradley."

"Hi, Mr. Bradley."

"Hi, England. It's nice to meet you."

"Now that we've been formally introduced, let's take some pictures so they won't be late for dinner."

"Yes, pictures."

After taking the pictures, England and Jay got in the rental car and headed down the street. Jay could not keep his eyes off England. He was admiring her beauty, while she thought he was the most handsome young man that she'd ever dated. In the midst of her staring, her phone rang. It was Gabby, informing her that they were going to stop by Matthew's house and take pictures and then they'd be on their way.

Matthew's parents took a lot of pictures and enjoyed meeting Gabby. They were so impressed with their son. He was graduating from high school and would be the first to go to college in their family. He had received several scholarships and was ready to pursue his dreams. He hoped that he could get enough education to fit into Gabby's family. He felt that they were not well matched at present because Gabby came from a wealthy family and his family was average. However, Gabby was not concerned about that right now. She knew that Matthew was a gentleman, and she trusted him. After the pictures, they headed downtown to meet England and Jay, hoping they weren't late.

England and Jay made it to the restaurant on time. The valet opened England's door to help her out, while Jay was accepting the parking ticket from the guy on his side. They walked into the restaurant and gave the maître d' Matthew's name. While he was looking up the name, Jay looked at England and smiled. She smiled back.

"Hey, did I tell you how beautiful you are this evening?"

"Yes, you did."

"Well, I'm telling you again. You are one gorgeous young woman. Thanks for allowing me to share this night with you."

"Thanks for inviting me to your prom."

"You are quite welcome."

The maître d' called Matthew's name and escorted them to the table.

"You made reservations for four, sir."

"Yes, the rest of the party is on their way."

"May I get you something to drink while you wait?"

"Yes, I would like a glass of water."

"And you, madam?"

"Iced tea with lemon."

"Coming right up."

"So, England, tell me about your boyfriends."

"You sure you want to hear about all 52?"

"What!"

"Shhhhh, not so loud."

"Well, you said 52," Jay said.

"I'm sure you've had just as many girlfriends."

"No, that's not true. I've only had about five or six in my lifetime."

"What, that's all?"

"Seriously, yes."

"Why so few?"

"I played sports year round and girls couldn't handle it," Jay said. "They wanted more than I could give them, or should I say more than I wanted to give."

"So, you were all about sports?"

"Yes, I love it."

"And now?"

"I still love it. I just wanted to go to the prom. But I didn't want to take any of them. Besides, I like you. I find you to be very attractive, England. I don't know how much of my time you would want if we start dating seriously."

"I don't know how much time I will be able to give you if we get serious," said England. "I have to study and go to cheering practice. I might even try out for the track team. As a matter of fact, we might be too busy for that type of relationship."

Jay was looking at England very curiously. As England spoke, she was looking Jay right in his eyes. She kept her steady stare until he gave in and looked away. Jay was flabbergasted with what England had said. He thought she would be glad to have him for a boy-friend. He was quiet for a minute. He was trying to come up with something that would take her by surprise, but he couldn't top that. He was sure she meant every word. Before Jay was able to speak, Gabby and Matthew came up, following the maître d'. Jay rose from his seat and kissed Gabby on the cheek. Gabby introduced Matthew to Jay. The boys shook hands, and then the maître d' pulled out Gabby's chair.

"How was the traffic?" asked Jay.

"Not so bad," said Matthew. "I took some detours to get us here."

"He sure did," added Gabby. "I thought we were lost, but he knew how to get us here without all the traffic."

"So, you know Atlanta pretty well, huh?"

"Pretty much."

"Gabby, you look nice tonight."

"Thanks, Jay."

"And England, you look beautiful as always. That color is definitely you."

"Thanks, Matthew. You look good, too, when you clean up."

They all laughed.

"So, Jay, I've seen your picture in the paper on numerous occasions," said Matthew. "Your stats are off the charts too. What does ASU's team look like this year?"

"I think we're going to have a winning team. I've met several tough guys coming from top high schools. I think we're going to have plenty of talent on the field this year. SIAC, here we come."

"Yeah, I hear that. What will you major in?"

"Law," Jay said, "I would like to be a corporate lawyer."

"Oh, that's a tough field to break into," Matthew said, "but you've got the right GPA, so you should be able to achieve it."

"What about you?" Jay asked.

"Although my options are open, I'm leaning towards theology," Matthew said. "I've been awarded several scholarships. I just need to make my mind up."

"So, ladies, we don't want to leave you out of the conversation," Jay said. "What is it you care to talk about?"

The waitress interrupted them, asking if they would like to order an appetizer. They decided on the stuffed mushroom and escargot. After the waiter took the appetizer and drink order, their conversation continued.

"Okay, ladies, what's new?" asked Matthew.

"Well, the museum is bringing in great art from around the world. The display will start next week," said Gabby.

"Hey, can we go as a group like we did last time?" asked Matthew.

"That was fun," said Gabby.

"I enjoyed lunch better," England said.

"England, I thought you enjoyed the museum."

"I did, Matthew. I just said I enjoyed lunch better. The conversation was great. The company was good. The food was excellent."

"Yeah, I enjoyed that too. Matthew, we'll let you set it up for us. Call everybody and plan on a meeting date."

"All right," Matthew said. "You know I am the planner. You're also welcome, Jay."

"Yes, please come and be prepared to share in the conversation."

"Well, thanks for the invitation," Jay said. "Just let me know the date and time."

"I am so ready to go to college. I can't wait. This summer is going to be interesting."

"What's going to happen this summer, Matthew?"

"I have to kiss Ms. B goodbye."

"Oh yeah, you're talking about the lady who gave you a lot of money for your college tuition."

"Yes, but every time I come home, I'll make sure I visit with them," said Matthew. "They have truly been a blessing. If it were not for them, I wouldn't have applied to school and I wouldn't have been so excited. I can't thank God enough."

"Hey, I can relate to that," Jay said. "I grew up with my mom and sister. Mr. Bradley stepped into my life and made it a success. He is my hero. Without him I wouldn't have come this far. I was supposed to be a statistic, coming from a single parent household. A person like me could have been written off a long time ago. But I guess God saw something in me that I didn't or couldn't see in myself."

"Well, you both are prime examples of God's work," said England. "He said He will never leave us nor forsake us."

The waitress came with the appetizers and was ready to take their entrée orders. England ordered shrimp and steak, Gabby ordered 8 oz. filet mignon, and the boys both ordered Porterhouse steak. The girls looked at them and laughed.

"What's wrong?" asked Jay.

"What's funny?" Matthew echoed.

"I can't believe you're going to eat all of that meat," said Gabby.

"That is such a huge quantity," said England. "Do you know the size of that thing?"

"Yes, 32 ounces."

"Okay, don't complain later about your stomach hurting."

"You all have time to change your order if you'd like."

"No, thanks."

"Okay."

The orders came and the steaks were huge. The boys looked at them and were ready to eat, but first they said the prayer. Gabby and England started eating, watching as the boys prepared their steak with all the fixings. They ate and talked at the same time. England was looking at how Jay cut his steak with a knife and then put the steak in his mouth with the knife. She was laughing on the inside. She couldn't believe he was able to eat that much. Maybe that's what football players do. Matthew was handling his steak as well. He was almost finished when the waitress came by to refill their glasses.

England noticed that a man had been watching them for at least the last 30 minutes. She looked around to see if anyone else was staring. She didn't notice anyone else. Gabby noticed England's awkward look. She too started looking around, observing her surroundings, and noticing the man staring at them. When Gabby looked again, she thought he was only watching Jay. England brought it to their attention.

"Hey, guys don't look right now, but I think we have an admirer. Or should I say Jay has an admirer. The white guy over at 9:00 is watching us like a hawk. He's been doing so for the last twenty to thirty minutes."

"Okay, let's look at him so he'll know that we're staring," Jay said. "But first let me finish this last piece of meat. Because if he comes over, I won't shake his hand while I'm eating, and I don't really want to be disturbed."

"I agree, let's finish our meal, and then give him some attention."

They finished all their food--all that they could possibly eat. The man was still looking at them off and on, as if he was waiting for the right moment to come over. The waitress asked them if they wanted dessert. They all said no. Jay complained that he was about to burst out of his shirt. Matthew asked for the check. The waitress said that the check had been taken care of. They asked by whom. The waitress pointed to the gentleman England was talking about. They nodded their heads to say thank you. He came over to introduce himself.

"Hi, my name is Jim Albright. I'm with the *Daily Times*."

"Nice to meet you, Mr. Albright," said Jay.

"I wanted to let you know that you're an awesome ball player, and I will be following your college career."

"Thanks. And thanks so much for picking up our bill."

"Not a problem. I see you all are on your way to the prom."

"Yes, we are."
"Well, have a good evening."
"Thanks," the kids said in unison.
They left a tip and went to their proms.

Chapter 21

England and Gabby

hree weeks went by. Gabby and England were enjoying pizza at Benigno's engulfed in conversation when Matthew and Jay walked up.

"England, this has been a crazy year. I never thought it would end like this."

"I agree. I thought we were going to the prom stag. But God allowed us to meet good people and enjoy the most important event of our senior year."

"I thought Senior Day was the most important event."

"No, girl you can skip by yourself. Who's going to know?"

"You are so right. Who will miss me?"

"Hey," said Jay.

England and Gabby were startled.

"Hi, didn't your momma tell you about sneaking up on people?"

"No, she told me to be quiet so I can eavesdrop on your conversation."

The boys grabbed a seat and sat down at the table next to the girls.

"So, what's up? What were you guys talking about?"

"This year has ended with some ups and downs," said Gabby.

"What happened?" asked Jay.

"Calvin is still sick, and he's not going to make graduation."

"Wow! Will the school send his diploma?" asked Matthew.

"I don't know. I suppose if they think his overall grades were passable—he had a lot of late homework assignments," said Gabby.

Jay looked on and listened, trying to figure out what they were talking about.

"I guess so. I don't know if I could walk in those shoes."

"What are you all talking about?" Jay finally asked.

"We're talking about one of our classmates who has HIV and has been home for months now. However, he already had enough hours to finish school last December," said England.

"He must be bright."

"Yes, he is really smart when it comes to those books."

"But he allowed life to take him by surprise," replied England.

"Yes."

"We have some kids at our school in the same shape," said Jay. "But they take their medicine, and you can't tell they have the virus."

"Yes, according to the statistics a lot of folks must still be having unprotected sex because the number of new HIV cases is increasing every day."

"Lord Jesus."

"You can say that again."

"This is one reason why we need more forums, workshops, and TV programs talking about teens and their outrageous behavior."

"I know exactly what you're saying," replied Matthew. "However, it's a difficult topic to discuss. The United States Government and everybody else are pushing it under the rug, as if it's no big deal."

"I don't think they're doing that," replied Jay. "I think parents need to enlighten themselves on what's going on in what I call the 'teen world.' They need to educate themselves as well as their kids."

"But do you want to leave it to the parents?" asked England. "HIV is an epidemic among teens. It's bigger than we can imagine. There are thousands of kids suffering with the virus. Some were born with it because they contracted it from their mothers, who contracted it from someone else. Others got it from sexual contact, homosexual activity, or drugs. Now they're passing it on to other people."

"When you talk about parents taking control and educating their kids, you've got to remember that a lot of parents are themselves lacking. They still need some guidance in their lives," replied Matthew.

"I can relate to that. Remember, England, when China said that her mom told her she has to beat the boys at their own game?"

"Yeah, that's a mother who needs help herself," said England.

"Since that day I've not seen China in school," said Gabby.

"The last time I talked with her, she said she was going to the doctor and they both were going to get an HIV test," replied England. "Come to think of it, she hasn't been in school since then."

"Maybe her test was positive."

"Maybe."

"Tell me something," Gabby said. "First of all, can we talk and be honest here?"

"Sure," the boys said in unison.

"Tell me, why are you guys so different from other guys?"

"Well, for me, I don't think I'm so different," said Matthew. "I am similar to them, but yet...different. I don't mess around with color. It's black and white for me."

"Explain," said Gabby.

"See, hues black and white are not mixed with anything to get their tone," Matthew went on. "They are who they say they are. There's no in between. When I look at color, color has a mixture or a combination of things. In other words, it's not true. For example, look at orange. What makes orange? Colors mixed together. I pick a girl based on how she carries herself. I observe her for days, maybe even months before I go speak to her. After I've collected enough data, I ask her one question. If she gets it wrong, I keep stepping. A lot of girls fall in the color scheme because they are not true."

"So, you play a game?" asked Gabby.

"No, it's not a game. Gabby, you remember the question I asked you."

"Yes, I remember. I always think about that question."

"What's the question?" asked Jay.

"Sorry, I can't share."

"What about you, Jay?" asked Gabby.

"I hadn't really had time to pick a girl before I met England. At my school, being a star athlete ensured that there were always girls. They would ask me out before I even had time to talk to them, to see if I wanted to go out. It was depressing at first, because I knew that those girls only wanted me because I was a star athlete."

"Wow upsetting," said Jay.

"I guess I could have worked a little harder to date more, but the guys would just sit around the locker room and talk about the girls like they were dogs. Then they would plaster a smile on their faces, trying to get up on some play. After about three or four months, if that long, they would be finished and done with her, and go on to the next girl."

"So, tell me, did your teammates pick on you?" asked Matthew.

"Of course," Jay said. "I had to go through hell. One guy was all in my face talking that smack that I wasn't getting any. I told him not to get in my face with that nonsense. Then here he came again. I picked him up by the scruff of the neck and threw him into the lockers. It took about five coaches to get me off of him."

"Dog, boy. You were angry!" said Gabby.

"Yeah, but since then I know exactly how to get under their skin," Jay said. "My mentor helped train my attitude. He really gives me a new way of looking at things. So, when jokers start talking that smack, I know how to delete myself out of the equation. I just say, 'Excuse me,' and walk away very cool, as if I'm in control of the moment."

"Good for you!"

"It took a lot of practice, but I have it down to a science now."

Jay took a deep breath.

"By now I know you've probably figured that I'm still a virgin at seventeen."

England, Gabby, and Matthew let out a sigh of relief.

"Well, join the team. It's okay. It's what we're supposed to hold onto until marriage," said Gabby.

"But people don't make a big deal out of losing their virginity."

"No, and they won't because it's not a big deal to those who have lost theirs."

"I'm sure we all have our reasons for holding on. We all know that the Bible speaks against fornication and that's one reason. But are there some other reasons? I'm not saying there should be. The Bible should be enough for us, but sometimes we think in the flesh," said Jay.

"For me, it's because there are so many diseases out there. It's just scary. I want to live a long healthy life. When I visited Calvin in the hospital, I saw what he was going through and that validated my decision even more to stay pure," said Gabby.

"I know that I've had sexual thoughts. I thought it was because my body was going through puberty, preparing the reproductive system. My thoughts probably came from watching videos when I was still trying to find out who I was and what I wanted to do in my life. In eighth grade I had to do a report for health class, so I started searching the internet looking for a good topic. As I searched, I discovered all types of diseases, and they had the pictures connected to the articles. That was very disturbing. I learned a lot from the internet. My parents never talked to me about sex or drugs. I taught myself using the internet," said Matthew.

"Being an athlete," said Jay, "I used to always get hit in certain places when we were playing without our gear. I knew most of the time I could find anything on the internet, so I relied on it. One time I wanted to know when to apply heat to an injury and when to apply cold, so I searched it. While I was on there, I decided to go to the website that talked about teens and sex. On this website they had everything broken down into categories. So I went to the category that said, 'Teens living with HIV.' I read a lot of articles that night and learned a lot from the teens who had posted comments. It was so horrifying that I couldn't sleep."

"It was that powerful?" asked England.

"Yes," Jay said. "I didn't know those kids. They were between the ages of 15 and 18. Some of them mentioned that they would never share that information because they would lose their friends and be in this world alone."

"That's why people continue to pass it on. They don't want to be ridiculed," Matthew continued. "They are afraid that they will no longer have friends if they tell."

"I know I'm a young man, and some think it's a shame that I'm still a virgin," said Jay, "but I found out those who are doing most of the talking ain't getting none either. I'm just straight up with who I am, and I don't care what the world thinks of me. They have to pretend to fit in the crowd, which is silly to me," Jay continued. "I have a sister who is in the ninth grade, and she is too 'grown-up.' I told my momma she needs to talk to her before she gets out of hand."

"Tell your mom to take her to the clinic. They will talk to her and show her the videos," said England.

"I didn't know they do that," said Jay.

"Yes, just call and ask."

"I'll tell her. If she doesn't have time to take her, I will."

"You should videotape her and show your mom," says Matthew.

"I should, because she thinks Lily is an angel, that she is totally innocent," said Jay.

"Well, she's at the age of innocence. We all are. We lack worldly experience," said England.

"I will be lacking for a while," said Jay.

They all laughed.

"Hey, this has been an interesting conversation, but I must depart from such beautiful young ladies and the old-fashioned dude."

They all laughed at Matthew.

"Yes, I guess we need to pay the tab and bounce too."

"Hey, I got the tab," said Matthew.

"Are you sure? We got money," said Gabby.

"Yeah, I know you're rich, but I got this tab," said Matthew.

"Hey man, let me help out," said Jay.

"Nah, I got it. You can pay the next one," said Matthew.

"All right."

They gave one another a hug and said their goodbyes. This conversation had been a long time coming, thought Gabby. She was more impressed with how Jay and Matthew were handling their friends on the matter. England was thinking that the conversation came up right on time. She believed the boys were honest regarding what they said this evening. If one of them was lying, they would find out later. But for now, they hadn't given any reason for the girls not to believe them. England was deep in thought when Gabby called her name.

"England. England!"

"What girl! Why are you screaming?"

"I was trying to get your attention. You are so deep in thought."

"Okay, you have my attention."

"I was just wondering what you thought about our conversation."

"I thought it was great," England said. "I just didn't get the color scheme strategy. But we asked questions that we were really thinking about. I learned something from each of you this evening."

"Did you think that Jay was still a virgin?"

"No, I thought he was probably going to be this wild person. But just looking at his body language and listening to his tone as he spoke, I knew he was not having sex with girls. But I also figured he probably

167

had tried it, since it was just sort of thrown in his face."

"Yes, well, you know it's not going to be any different at college. Girls are going to try him. The scenery will just be different."

"Well, Gabby, this is going to be a test for all of us. College is a whole different world. No parents, no curfew, we will be solely in control of our lives. And with God's help, we will be all right."

"We've got to really keep ourselves in check. We are going to help each other be accountable."

"Yes, please put me back in line when you see I'm headed to damnation."

"Hey, we'll be okay. Just don't take these boy-girl relationships too seriously. College is just a temporary stop in our lives. We may need to go back over our notes in dealing with the opposite sex. Boys can mess up your mind if you let them get too close."

"This is scary, but it feels good to know we have a lot of challenges ahead of us, but we know the way to go."

"We just cannot lose sight.

We won't. We'll find a church that'll continue to teach us the Word."

"I agree. I don't want to miss church. Things may start happening that I'm not equipped to handle on my own."

"Hey, we'll be fine. We won't get too involved with campus life. Maybe go to a party every now and then."

Gabby looked at England.

"Maybe."

The music played softly as the girls rode home in complete silence, both lost in their thoughts.

Chapter 22

England and Gabby

Engalnd and Gabby are lying across England's bed reminiscing about their past experiences. This has been a big year for the girls. They look back at their lives as if it was a play viewed through the lens of a camera, to capture the events that had taken place.

In the first scene, England, Gabby, Calvin, and Ken had been a part of each other's lives since middle school. They remembered the deep crushes they had on the boys and vice versa.

In the second scene, they looked back on the times when China and her friends didn't like them at all. By the time they got into high school, everybody was aware of their animosity. They all made it known that they had no love for each other. They had problems for many years with China, and therefore they expected it. It wasn't until this year that they examined the situation in the Christian organization meeting. The question the coach asked had made them seek spiritual guidance. China had basically told them that she envied them because of their character and conduct. This was an eye-opening statement that led the girls to believe that China had been suffering from low self-esteem all along.

In the third scene, new people had entered their lives. England had met Nikki, Tracy, and Jay, while Gabby had met Matthew, Elijah, and Sarah. When you combine their friends, England and Gabby had a new set of friends with similar beliefs. All were grounded in the Word, except Nikki and Tracy. However, they were still trying to learn.

In the fourth scene, England and Gabby had gone to two proms.

They did not imagine they would even go to one, especially with a guy. They thought that since they were Christians and had decided to remain virgins, they would have a hard time finding a date and interacting with their male counterparts. They knew they were doing the right thing by delaying sex. However, they did not become popular because of it. They knew they were outcasts. At one time it bothered them, because they didn't have a lot of friends. But with their parents' guidance, a firm sense of self-worth, and spiritual growth, they realized that being true to themselves was more important than having a lot of friends who were engaged in unhealthy behaviors.

In the fifth scene, while going through their teen experiences, they learned a lot about themselves as well as others. Every person who walked in and out of their lives had a lesson to teach them. Some dropped off the good and some dropped off the bad. Through their challenges, they learned how to be good decision-makers. They had learned from their mistakes as well as the mistakes of others— mistakes that would impact them the rest of their lives. As they looked back, they could see that being a virgin was not so bad after all.

In the final scene, they endured the pain of knowing that one of their friends was HIV positive. His life had changed forever. Would he go to college, or would he be too sick to attend? They thought about Nikki, China, Ken and others who may also have the virus. Ken said he had been tested. What were China's results? Did Nikki ever get tested? They wondered if they'd done all they could do to help Calvin, Ken, Nikki, and China.

Gabby and England had a plan, and they were on their way to greater experiences. They were looking forward to experiencing the college life. They were ready to embark on their next phase of life, the four-year journey through college. They'd been trained by good parents and led by the grace of God. Although they would continue to have some challenges, they feared no evil, because they knew that where they went, God would also go.

I hope you read the second book, living life on a college campus.

Readers Group
Discussion Questions

1. Gabby went to a party, but there was no adult supervision, so she
    called her mom. What would you have done?

2. As a Christian, do you think England and Gabby should have re-
    solved the issue with China sooner?

3. What effect do you think the "girlie" magazines and other forms
    of entertainment had on Calvin's and Ken's actions and attitudes?

4. If you thought Nikki should get help but feared you were going to
    break her confidence, what would you do?

5. What type of spiritual and emotional support did England and
    Gabby give Calvin, Ken, and Nikki?

6. Do you think Ken became aware of his convictions and tried to
    build a better relationship with God? How are you learning to
    stand up for your convictions and say no to things you know are
    wrong?

7. HIV is a growing epidemic among teens. What way would be the
    best way to educate your peers?

8. Since HIV is on the rise on college campuses, do you think it
    should be mandatory for all incoming freshmen to take an HIV-
    101 class, or should it be a part of freshmen orientation?

9. What helps you overcome your fears?

10. Who do you talk to when you have a tough decision to make?

11. There were times when England got angry. What advice would you have given her to deal with her anger?

12. Gabby comes from a wealthy family, but Matthew does not. If they continue to date each other, what will be some of their challenges?

www.ingramcontent.com/pod-product-compliance
Lightning Source LLC
Chambersburg PA
CBHW050406030726
47503CB00006B/2048